ON

THE EDGE

OF REASON

ON
THE EDGE
OF REASON

A NOVEL BY

Miroslav Krleža

A NEW DIRECTIONS PAPERBOOK

Originally published as *Na rubu pameti* in 1938.
Published by arrangement with Athenäum Verlag.
First published in Great Britain by Quartet Books Ltd., 1989.

First published as New Directions Paperbook 810 in 1995
and reissued with a new introduction as NDP1567 in 2023
(ISBN 978-0-8112-2204-4)
Manufactured in the United States of America

Library of Congress Cataloging-in-Publication Data
Krleža, Miroslav, 1839–
[No rubu pameti. English]
On the edge of reason / Miroslav Krleža ;
translated from the Croatian by Zora Depolo.
p. cm.
ISBN 978-0-8112-1306-6
I. Depolo, Zora. II. Title.
PG1618.K69N33 1995 95-37589
891.8'235—dc20

2 4 6 8 10 9 7 5 3 1

New Directions Books are published for James Laughlin
by New Directions Publishing Corporation
80 Eighth Avenue, New York 10011

CHAPTERS

INTRODUCTION

In Poe's *The Imp of the Perverse* (1845), a man pulls off a perfect crime—to be precise, he pulls off a perfect murder, which he considers so masterful that it can't go unreported. He develops the need to tell someone about it—to tell anyone or everyone—and, driven by this need, finds himself dashing to the cops to make a full confession. In the century after Poe's story, the phrase "the imp of the perverse" came to mean the urge to do exactly the wrong thing at the wrong time, the imp-ulse (sorry) to self-sabotage and self-destruction.

Poe's imp puts a stop to his tale, but the impetus (sorry again) to speak against all reason—contra all common sense and advisement—is what starts so many examples of what I'm going to call, because I can't help myself, Imp Fiction. This genre I just made up out of the perverse inversion of Poe's poetics includes fiction whose plot is set in motion by an outburst—usually a remark attributed to one of its characters or delivered by its narrator within quotations. In other words, Imp Fic, or, in a word, Impfic, occurs when a guy (yes, typically a guy, used to speaking and used to being listened to) says something he doesn't have to and perhaps really shouldn't and proceeds to suffer the consequences—often through his remark being, by his own account, misinterpreted, even willfully misinterpreted.

Two great Impfics come to mind from my own tradition: Saul Bellow's *Him with His Foot in His Mouth* (1984), in which a single insult spontaneously delivered by a male professor to a female colleague echoes through their subsequent careers, and Philip Roth's *The Human Stain* (2000), in which a Black professor passing as Jewish makes a quip about absent students that's racially construed and unravels his existence. It's telling that recent American literature sets these Impfics in colleges and universities, especially in their humanities departments, the primary precincts for speech policing in this country, where horny, entitled, and newly unparented youth meet their cultural inheritance and, before seeking to understand it, seek to demolish it.

But if Impfic, like all fiction, must be judged on its aesthetics, its aesthetics must be judged as inextricable from its politics. In a sense, the greater the consequences of speaking up, the greater the power of speech, which is why Impfic's true heyday was the Soviet twentieth century, where it comprised much of the best literature of dissidence. Impfic, a genre predicated on subversion, was necessarily published underground, in books that circulated in samizdat if not merely in manuscript between the drawers, illegalized, seized, banned, and often destroyed along with their creators. Perhaps the most classic example of Soviet Impfic is *The Joke* (1967), a novel that announces its ambitions in its title, which might also have been intended as a type of preemptive (self-) defense. The fiction debut of the Czechoslovak author Milan Kundera, who back in his student days in the 1950s found himself expelled from the Communist Party, *The Joke* could not be more straight-faced in its setup: a man named Ludvík has a crush on a woman named Markéta and they strike up a flirtatious correspondence—rather, Ludvík flirts and Markéta treats his entreaties as opportunities for ideological engagement. Sent to an indoctrination course by the

Party she serves, Markéta writes to Ludvík praising the course's discussions, the group calisthenics and group singing, and, as she puts it, the general overall "healthy atmosphere." Ludvík responds with a postcard that reads in full: "Optimism is the opium of the people! A healthy atmosphere stinks of stupidity! Long live Trotsky!" His entire life after he posts that card constitutes *The Joke*'s dark punchline: he's booted from school, loses the ability to work, and is sent for hard labor and reeducation, a proleptic plot that foreshadows how Kundera himself was eventually stripped of his Czechoslovak citizenship and forced to find refuge in France.

Among the contenders for the earliest and most purely entertaining work of Soviet Impfic is the novel you hold in your hands: Miroslav Krleža's *On the Edge of Reason*—a book that could only have been written and published at the edge of *un*reason, which is to say, on the eve of the Second World War in Yugoslavia. A moderately successful and moderately influential and moderate-in-pretty-much-every-way lawyer from Zagreb is our hero and narrator. Along with his wife and a bevy of Party notables and functionaries, he is attending a dinner—a drunken symposium— at the vineyard estate of a Director-General.

Amid slurps of intoxicating grape, the Director recounts an evening at the close of the First World War when bandits, presumably gone AWOL from the Imperial Army, broke into his cellars and attempted to steal his wine, a theft he prevented by shooting them dead. Defending his private property on the eve of its nationalization, the Director picked up a carbine and killed four of them: "two were shot in the head on the spot, the one near the vine arbor got two bullets in his left lung, and the last one, who fell near the fence, bled to death after the artery in his neck had been hit," in the reportorial translation of Zora Depolo.

As the Director reminisces, the reader gets the sense—and the narrator confirms the sense—that this isn't the first time he's re-hashed his "exploit," and yet something about this occasion is different. Perhaps what's different is that the Director's glory-days story has now come wrapped and beribboned within the containing story of a novel, or else it's that at some point in the stroll down memory lane another guest arrives at the party: a guest unnamed, unmentioned, incorporeal.

Call him, if you will, the Imp, who wells up within the narrator and spurs him, our moderate everyman, into externalizing his interior monologue by saying: "it was all a crime, a bloody thing, moral insanity"—a tripartite phrase that appears in the novel in quotation marks, because like any effective spell or benediction or prayer for the dead, it's a phrase that's pronounced aloud.

> By pure chance, this naïve phrase in my soliloquy coincided with a pause between two sentences uttered by the Director-General—dead silence. And because of that dead silence, special significance was attached to every individual word I said. [...]
>
> The Director-General—his belly protruding, with pouting lips, with horizontal wrinkles on his low stiff forehead and with a burning match in his right hand—watched everything from under his pince-nez while lighting his third Havana. He then stopped for a while to inhale through his cigar and, holding it half lit in his hand between the left index and middle finger, leaned toward me and, expressing sudden surprise as if wondering what I had in mind, asked me what was bloody and what crime was in question.
>
> "Everything: your wine, the four dead men you described as mad dogs. You see, you've been telling us about this all evening. Well, that's it ..."
>
> "How do you mean? I don't get you," said the Director-General, still expecting me to explain what I had muttered from behind my teeth so as to enable him to breathe two or three times at peace through his Havana before the match was extinguished in his hand.

"How do you mean—morally insane? What crime? What is bloody about it?"

"Well, you have been telling us about it, boasting of having shot four men. Anybody can shoot a man if the opportunity arises. But only individual persons prone to crime can boast of murder. That is what I mean by a morally insane situation."

"Then you approve of the burglary? If that's so, I regret not having shot you too, as the fifth."

And so begins—and so continues—the famous spiral, the infamous plummet. Refusing to recant and apologize, refusing to use his overindulgence in the Director's booze as an excuse, our hero's tale becomes a tallying of losses: like an attorney handling a bankruptcy, his own, he notes the loss of his wife, his employment, his reputation, his status, and eventually his freedom ...

Krleža's account of this fall from grace is tantamount to a fantasy of his counterexistence: this is what the author's own fate might've been had he been Czechoslovak or Polish, and certainly if he'd been Russian or Ukrainian or a Muslim from one of the stans or anywhere a Jew.

Like his narrator, Krleža (1893–1981) was a throwback of sorts, a Jesuit-educated child whose mind was formed by the cosmopolitanism of the Austro-Hungarian Empire, which turned to dust— to dust and to Titoism—right at the start of his long career (his first major publications came in the final year of the Dual Monarchy, 1918). But unlike the "top-hatted man," the *homo cylindriacus*, who babbles throughout this book, Krleža was both a serious Marxist and a serious artist, an innovator of the language once known as Serbo-Croatian and now just plain Croatian. Above all, he was an expert in how to survive: how to survive the Eastern front as a soldier in the Imperial Army; how to survive being expelled by the Communist Party in 1939 due, officially at least, to his opposition to the doctrines of Socialist Realism, and his refusals to support the Purges; how to survive the Nazification of Croatia, the Serbian Chetniks, and Tito, to become a leading bureaucrat at the Yugoslav Academy of Sciences and Arts, the head of the Yugoslav Institute for Lexicography, and the president of the Yugoslav Union of Writers—all while publishing over forty volumes of fiction, poetry, plays, and memoirs.

His was a laureled career in the single censorious, sometimes-Moscow-aligned-and-sometimes-not country where, if you had certain connections and ethnic protections, you could let your inmost imp speak. It was a mark of Krleža's humanism that he understood this privilege as a responsibility to give voice to the imps of others—especially to those of his brother writers being persecuted in points further east. 1938, the year *On the Edge of Reason* was published, was the final year of the Stalinist show trials, and the year that Osip Mandelstam perished in the gulag, for the crime of writing a half-humorous poem that, basically, called the mustachioed Georgian who ran the USSR dumb and clumsy and fat.

A man of conviction, a man of pride, Krleža had the luck to express the imps of his age without compromising either his principles or his colleagues. He protected those he could, and in his official capacities neither issued nor consented to any denouncements. In sum, his career, and his integrity, were damn near miraculous—they would still constitute a miracle in contemporary America—and his imp didn't hesitate to acknowledge as much, not through boasting or bragging or rubbing noses in the liberties taken, but through this brief, harrowing, charmingly witty book, a masterly novel whose preeminent folly is that it "dare[s] to oppose human folly."

— JOSHUA COHEN

TRANSLATOR'S NOTE

With few exceptions, the original spelling of Croatian proper names has been retained throughout this volume. The following key will help the reader in pronouncing them:

c = ts	as in lots	lj = li	as in stallion
č and ć = ch	as in change	dj = j	as in major
š = sh	as in marsh	i = ee	as in feet
ž = s	as in pleasure	e = e	as in net
j = y	as in yes	u = oo	as in soon
	a = a	as in father	

ON

THE EDGE

OF REASON

1

ON

HUMAN FOLLY

At night, when I hold conversations with myself, I cannot logically justify my constant preoccupation with human folly.

Whether human folly is the work of God or not, it does not diminish in practice. Centuries often elapse before one human folly gives place to another, but, like the light of an extinguished star, folly has never failed to reach its destination. The mission of folly, to all appearances, is universal. Folly is a celestial force, like gravitation or light or water. Folly is much enamored of itself, and its self-love is unlimited. Folly is clad in distinctions and professions, titles and ranks. Folly is decorated with gold chains like a Lord

Mayor. It rattles spurs and waves censers. Folly wears a top hat on
its highly learned head, and this top-hatted folly is a form I have
studied fairly closely. Indeed, I have had both the honor and the
good fortune to spend my whole humble, insignificant life as a modest member of the middle class, so modest as to be almost invisible,
among top-hatted people.

Our domestic, autochthonous, so to speak national and racial top-
hatted man, *homo cylindriacus*, who, as a rule, is at the head of some
man-established institution, thinks of himself, in the glamour of his
civic dignity, as follows: On behalf of the seven thousand doctors
of all sorts, I stand at the head of my own branch of learning as its
most outstanding representative, the most worthy of respect. Every
word I have uttered up to this day has been right and proper in my
highly learned dissertations, printed by our honorable academy. I
am the chairman of twenty-three societies. In fact, the fairy guard-
ing the cradle of every newborn infant predicted that I should be a
patron and lawyer, honorary chairman and president, initiator, ide-
ologist, funeral orator and speaker at unveiling ceremonies, and
eventually have a bronze statue of myself erected in one of our
parks. In the shadow of my top hat I have enjoyed the dignity of
one whose name appears in our *Who's Who* followed by four full
lines of the titles and subtitles of my civil-service functions. I am a
man who, on principle, has lived my orderly and honorable life
within my income, without debts, without moral, civic, or other
stain, without political suspicion, as an irreproachable patriot, as
open as a tradesman's books, accessible for inspection at any time,
polite, composed, clear, helpful, a model both to myself and to my
fellow citizens, a model citizen and toiler, a good husband who has
never slept with anybody except his own wife, whom he promptly,
during the first night of a happy marriage, made the mother of a

future learned doctor and future chairman or future wearer of a top hat, for the Lord commanded: Be born, learned doctors, and beget future learned doctors, for that is why the universe was created, i.e., that we, wearers of top hats, might multiply.

Human intelligence today is but nervous restlessness, or rather neurasthenic fussing amid the postdiluvian conditions of reality. We neurotic individuals are surrounded by dullards, landlords, owners of soda-water factories, honorable citizens and petit-bourgeois folk wearing bowlers and felt hats as they attend one another's funerals. Our top-hatted man is a model patriot, a member of the central committee of such and such a party, a city alderman, a town councilor, a factory owner, a benefactor and public worker who gives expression to his clever ideas in his party organ. His speech is allegorical. He protests publicly against motor transportation, yet lacks the true citizen's courage to revolt against military parades. After the whole globe has been in flames, after who-knows-how-many-dozen European cities have been devastated in the thunderstorm that has shaken Europe like an old piece of torn newspaper, and after the whole of Asia has been plunged into bloodshed, plague, fire, ruin, and catastrophe like a blasted stone-quarry, our *homo cylindriacus* protests against the use of "motor transport."

In the revolt against "motor transport," hearing the walls of his own house crack, the roof over his head shake, and the glasses in the dining-room cupboard rattle, our top-hatted man protests against contemporary reality on chivalrous grounds: he lives within the golden frame of an antiquated oleograph in which armored knights fight dragons in tournaments.

Enter into such a gold-framed outlook on life as that, try to explain to this man that his bourgeois logic has frail foundations, and what would he tell you in his turn? Either that you are morally corrupt, or someone working for a foreign power with the task of undermining our civilization, or, at best, that you are not right in your head.

For many years I lived in this stinking menagerie of a world, practically deaf and dumb, hidden and withdrawn into myself like a snail, a perfect mollusk. For years on end I contemplated human folly, vaguely realizing how a strange, obscure inner force appears behind various human actions, obstructing the individual in every movement, preventing people from living a full and straightforward life, a dangerous force poisoning and corroding them. This daily spectacle of human folly, as I saw it, was a natural phenomenon: "Man stood up on his hind legs, started to walk like a biped, and folly trailed behind him like a shadow. Folly, the sister of darkness, would have the biped return again to his quadruped relatives in the natural world. Thus folly prevents man from soaring upward in the direction of the stars, just as gravitation prevents him from flying."

In reality, I liked people. Indeed, I forgave them. I admired man's abilities, and when human folly made its appearance and diverted some wonderful achievement of man's will or enthusiasm to itself, dragging it in the mud, soiling it with filthy language, I interpreted the collapse of man's noble endeavor quite naturally, in well-meaning and conciliatory fashion: "If birds fall down exhausted and do not fly forever, why should human beings incessantly worry about their own dignity?" Or: "The individual who wants to elevate himself above his fellow citizens is like a wheel on a muddy road: it gets on, but it also gets dirty."

Human folly is an obscure force. It is the chaotic force of the primeval matter within us that human beings have not yet mastered but that they will, nevertheless, undoubtedly subdue eventually, and in this lies the meaning of human progress: the level of the different civilizations is in reverse proportion to the extent of human folly.

Up to the age of fifty-two I lived the dull and monotonous life of an average bourgeois, owning a carriage and wearing a top hat. I lived the life of an orderly good-for-nothing among a whole crowd of neat, gray good-for-nothings. Bored by the so-called performance of my own futile trifling duties, I went for thirty-five-hundred afternoon walks as far as the brickkiln or the cottage in the park on the outskirts of the city. I had quiet and unutterably monotonous intercourse with my lawful wife, and we had three girls, three stupid geese. I had a fairly respectable income as legal adviser to an industrial organization and to Domaćinski's enterprises and cartels. In brief: as regards myself and my life, my private as well as my public one, there was nothing to differentiate them from the ordinary, gray and impersonal lives adopted by thousands and thousands of bourgeois good-for-nothings all over our beloved country and traceable in all the innumerable patriotic civilizations on our planet.

I inherited from one of my distant relatives a very nice vineyard with a wooden summer cottage. I lived a dull family life with my wife, the daughter of a mediocre druggist from a provincial town who ruined the digestion of a whole generation with his herb tea but who, from the profits on that tea, had built three three-storied houses in our town. I myself lived in a beautiful, sunny, very respectable apartment with a balcony in one of those three-storied houses built on the proceeds of the digestive tea. The house was my own property because the druggist had given it to me as a token of his special affection. I was on visiting terms with some senior officials of the civil service who were my wife's relatives. Living like a householder and civil servant, I mixed with civil servants and householders of the same type—never, of course, meddling in local vul-

gar politics. Devoid of any particular passions, I listened to other
people talking about wars, fighting, adventures, big plans, and, generally, about big things and events. And so I spent my life in the
main listening to other people, in smoking, and in sleeping till nine
o'clock on Sundays and half-past seven on weekdays: nine hours at
least to rest my nerves and ensure a good and quiet digestion.

For many years I listened to talk about painting because my wife
had been a student of art for three years. No one knows why, for
she had practically no talent for painting. Still, she had a liking
for it, visited art exhibitions and bought paintings, and painters, in
return, honored my house with their visits. So there were long discussions in our house about painting in general, about individual
paintings and their sale, and, sporadically, about the art of painting
as such. Also, there was much talk about music, as it was discovered
that my elder daughter Agnes had a beautiful mezzo-soprano voice
and my wife pushed her on to the conservatory. While Agnes was
studying singing, preparing for the great career of a coloratura,
everybody in the house talked about opera, concerts, art. As my wife
was, considering our limited and backward circumstances, a cultured
and highly refined soul, and as I was in my turn born into this
world a naively hospitable man, my house was always crowded with
people. I liked guests and derived pleasure from my sociability, always being prepared to do other people some service. As a man, so
it seemed to me, I was in the main respected and liked more or less
by everybody.

In our small town there was gossip and slander on all sides, as in
all backwaters that want to play the role of capital cities, straining
themselves beyond their capacities. But, as far as I could gather
until I was fifty-two, no one ever heard a disparaging or malicious
statement about me. I was, in fact, quite nameless and invisible, so
discreet that nobody ever took any notice of my existence.

Nobody ever said that I had stolen anything from anybody: taken a silver spoon or robbed a cupboard. Nobody could allege that I had even eaten anything that belonged to anyone else, that I had pushed my way to a better or more profitable post at somebody else's expense. In the ridiculous whirl of our local folly, nobody ever smeared my name. As for that venereal disease that I contracted in first youth, hardly anybody knew about it. Except for that, there was nothing special in my early life. Even if this shameful experience had been known, it would have been a rather mild thing these days to launch against a popular and more or less respected citizen who wears a top hat, holds a prominent position, has a rich wife, possesses several houses in the main streets, has his own summer residence, and his own current accounts with solid banks in the center of town. Only later, after the storm broke around me and overnight I became the talk of the town, did I learn that I was a diseased pervert who had infected his own wife, that I was a cuckold, that my wife had had a lover for seven years, that I was a lecher, as I myself had admitted, and that even my own children were not mine. All this I heard after thirty years' silence about me. I appeared to be a completely different person from the individual conceived both by myself and by my closest friends throughout my life. By the time I began soberly to find out what had been happening to me, I saw in the mirror a decrepit old man with pouches under his eyes and bad teeth, a ridiculously protruding stomach, a thick neck and a double chin, the sad features of a bald, fat, dull, lazy man with a child's wooden sword in his hand, idiotically convinced that the fragile splinter was a rapier of pure moral determination that could be used to defend the national flag and honor against an entire petty, backward, and ridiculous civilization.

After a short period in the civil service, when I resigned as *chef de cabinet* to a feeble-minded man under a confused elective gov-

ernment and took the job of legal adviser to various industrial
concerns, basin factories, and sawmills, I spent my whole life preoccupied with other people's worries, splitting my not particularly
talented or well-organized head over other people's problems. I
loved the people about me persistently and selflessly, like a genuine
Samaritan, and, explaining my failures or unpleasant experiences
with people in the light of a lasting sympathy for those who suffer,
I derived comfort and compensation from a mild, practically Christian well-meaningness. If somebody cheated me into signing a bill
of exchange, on principle I would never get angry; moreover, I
never refused to sign another bill for such a scoundrel; I could always find some good, even praiseworthy feature of that particular
person as an excuse to prove that my experience with the promissory
note had betrayed only "a moment of weakness." "People are like
that," I used to say, silently reconciling myself to my fundamental
idea of charity—that one should love people because they are more
foolish than wicked. I believed somewhere deep down in myself
that no one has—over the long centuries of human experience—
ever discovered a remedy for human folly, and that it will still remain as it is today, i.e., semihuman and semifoolish, for a good long
time in the confusion around and within us.

Observing people with intense curiosity, I have often noticed how
they slander one another out of an incomprehensible but profound
need as strong in man as the force of gravity: an obscure force dragging him downward to the earth, into the mud. People persecute
one another and feel themselves persecuted by actions, by looks, by
speech. They sniff at each other distrustfully, like beasts. In fact,
people are only two-legged animals. They steal one another's ideas
and money, as monkeys in the jungle steal nuts from one another,
and when they have had enough of stealing and belching over their
foods, they go off, humming, waltzing, pissing in the underground

pissoirs of their filthy nightclubs where, from a distance, one can vaguely hear the strumming of the orchestra, as if to suggest: everything is all right with us, we have been satisfied through other people's suffering, everybody is kind to us, we are drunk, praise be to God.

Warm flesh wrapped in cloth and isolated from nature is set up on its hind legs in church, in the courtroom, on the stage, in the pulpit, in the chair, in pissoirs, in inns, in barracks. This warm flesh is dressed according to the mysterious rules of a great variety of historical costumes, classified according to sacrosanct castes, forced into a social mold and welded by the infernal machine of the state. The wretched human flesh is completely lost in the endless stream of unsolved problems; it cannot find a way out of the confusion and, separated into individuals, it is exclusively aware of its own flesh, forgetting the similar fleshiness of its fleshy neighbor. And so, from fear and foolishness, each bites the other's throat, turned into animals by fright and terrified in face of the dark. People are filled by their upbringing with superstitions, prejudices, and lies as if stuffed with straw. People play roles like puppets, as if wound up by other people, to an alien music that is absolutely incomprehensible and unintelligible to them. People revolve in the mindless circle of the so-called social round. Like riders on a genuine merry-go-round on the fairground, these riders on the wooden horses of social prejudice are convinced that they are galloping at an incredible speed within the closed circle of "success." When, from time to time, such a merry-go-round breaks down and the poor perplexed riders unexpectedly find themselves off the track, the infuriated careerists fail to adjust themselves to a life without a wooden horse. I have not yet had an opportunity to meet a single so-called clever and normal man bold enough to live his life on his own, without his business correspondence, without his office with its spittoon and seal; in brief, without

prejudices and without faith in wooden gods. Army officers after
lost wars, without horses and swearing; bankrupt bankers without
bank credits; singers without voices; dismissed officials, rejected
politicians, all those harlequins from the fairground, like shipwrecked people after a flood, float down the stream of prejudices to
rubbish dumps, dismissing from their minds the essence of their human nature. These straw puppets believe that the carnival had a
tragic end only because the wind had blown away their clownish
caps. Had this, by chance, occurred to other maskers, it would have
been a laughing matter for them. People always rejoice at other
people's disasters, forgetting that other people's trouble is their own.
In accordance with the classical dictum that all human weaknesses
are in fact elements of the secret humanity that makes man a miserable creature worthy of sympathy, I have always had the weakness
of sympathizing with everything that is human.

People deceive one another, tell lies to one's face, and are duped
by flattery and transparently insincere courtship. To them this all
honestly seems incomparably bolder than telling the naked truth.
People are egocentric, for they are unsatisfied and afraid of hunger;
they are ill-humored because they have been humiliated and hurt;
they are unfair, of course, but other people in their turn are not fair
to them; they are unhappy, scarred, embittered, in rags; they snore
underneath smelly feather quilts, envying each other on account of a
cup of coffee, a clean pillowcase, a new bicycle, fussing about every
trifle like jackdaws on a branch, squabbling—dialectically, of course
—as to which of them, now devouring the carrion of an unknown
hero, has the priority to treat himself to the man's eye.

One ought to like people, be helpful and obliging, be a hospitable host with a pleasant smile as sweet as marzipan in the window
of a confectioner's shop on New Year's Eve. This is what I have
preached as a social principle, and over the years I have also be-

haved according to this fundamental directive. One should welcome
people with outstretched arms and an open door. One should accept
people wholeheartedly, directly, spontaneously, be witty, cheer them
up if they are despondent, treat them well, buy fish, mayonnaise,
game, jelly, wine, tobacco, cheese, and subtropical fruit; one should
come back home in a cheerful mood carrying parcels, bottles; enter
warm, heated, well-lit rooms where richly set tables stand ready.
That is what I have always thought to be good and that is why I
cultivated my sociability and entertained in my house whole crowds
of scoundrels and dullards in endless succession. . . . One should
listen to other people's silly talk all night, let oneself be bored by
other people's self-love; show appreciation of other people's jokes;
listen to the dull, untalented playing of dilettantes. That is what I
used to tell myself, and that is how I actually ruined a whole life by
following my own autosuggestive instructions, a slave to my own
easygoing nature, ready to render any kind of service, a selfless,
good-humored, self-denying, and somewhat stupid moron, considered by his so-called friends to be a naive and rather tedious bore in
whose house there wasn't much fun but the food was quite good and
—almost always—rather good wine was served. Amid the clouds of
smoke, the fumes of alcohol, the foolish self-assertions, ill-bred im-
pertinences, and malicious slander, there gradually accumulated in
my mind over the years a feeling of satiety, disgust, and some undefined but nevertheless disturbing restlessness that, in relation to certain people, took the form of testy irritability. From time to time it
seemed to me too stupid to waste whole nights with babblers persistently repeating every night one and the same thing about various
political parties, party slanders and intrigues, constitutions, battles,
in endlessly tedious cackling and nonsensical affectation. In fact,
even previously I had noticed obvious symptoms of old age among
relatively young people worrying ill-humoredly about bad days to

come: complete lack of enthusiasm for generous and unselfish feelings, abrupt concealing of personal convictions, an unusually well-developed feeling of self-love, and, especially, for property: This is "my roof," "my knowledge," "my wife," "my conviction," "my book," "my income"—in general, "everything is mine." And I wondered what would become of those young gentlemen, our future "intellectuals" and "torchbearers," in a decade or two when, as young men, they delivered such stuttering monologues exaggerating the importance of even the most insignificant disturbances of "their" digestions. That was the question I asked myself, slightly suspicious of these babbling children of intellectuals who were themselves babblers, my schoolmates who had already produced the next senile generation of dancing doctors, famous lawyers, and lab assistants in veterinary clinics and asylums. I had often noticed that behind their masks people were actually unhelpful, cold, brutally indifferent toward everything that at the moment did not fall within the sphere of their immediate interest. They were narrow-minded, tedious, self-assertive, slandering others in incredible blind ignorance, failing to fulfill their obligations, to pay their debts, behaving like blind monkeys driven by their physical urges, not particularly clever, full of prejudices, vanity, and ambition. In such moods of clear-sighted depression, I would break away from the noise of humanity, for at times the atmosphere became too stifling in that stable with those two-footed cud-chewing beasts. Both the stable and the people stink, but it is warm inside the stable. In solitude, everything is empty. We know very well what there is under other people's tails, but we cannot live without sniffing. . . .

2

DINNER PARTY IN
DOMAĆINSKI'S VINEYARD

Had I not come to a turn in this account that could be described as
a fatal one, according to a mysterious law of human folly, in all
probability I would have spent my whole life overwhelmed by my
own contradictions—inert, lazy, slightly embittered, and fairly stupid, as life is when talking in taverns to silly babblers, or even to
friends, discussing the migration of peoples, battles, religions, books,
crocodiles, and especially the healing effects of mallow tea, trout,
and sharks. In the life of every individual human being there is a
time termed by novelists "fatal," and I had such a fatal experience
that fall. It was about two years ago. At present, I no longer remem-

ber the immediate cause that led to it, but everything started simply because I had ventured to say aloud what I had on my mind at that dramatic moment. My idea expressed was neither important nor particularly original. Similar thoughts had in fact been buzzing in my head in swarms for years. As I see things today, after everything that has taken place in the meantime, those thoughts had been the common daily occurrence with every one of my fellow citizens. The sole difference was that none of them would have thought of announcing such thoughts in public. People are not so silly as not to know what is and what is not permissible. No one among us is so stupid and naive as to admit anything courageously in public. And it applies in this case, too—unless, of course, one has never violated the Ten Commandments.

We are all masks and hide behind them. Although this is only wise, everybody feels the need to strip off the mask for a moment at least, to give vent to his most intimate feelings. But that a single word can disturb a whole life, detaching it like a balloon from the ground, that one word can soar in the air together with a fifty-two-year-old sybarite, separate him from a certain group of druggists, executives, and bourgeois society, and disappear with him in the fogs and distances, would have seemed fairly incredible to me, in fact something to be staged, had I not experienced it myself, had it not been my life now for two full years, in the glamour of a pathetic and, one could even say, almost heroic gesture.

At a dinner party in the vineyard of Director-General Domaćinski, on the veranda of his summer house, besides Mrs. Domaćinski, a talkative Viennese who, at the beginning of her social career, was a confectioner selling cakes in a café in Vienna, there was my wife Agnes, sitting next to a baritone. The latter was my eldest daughter's singing teacher (and, as I subsequently heard, had for seven years been my wife's lover, and at the moment was getting ready to become her legitimate husband as well). At the table covered with a white tablecloth were also several representatives of our elite: *homo cylindriacus, vir doctus magnificus* together with his son, who was a doctor of philosophy and an assistant professor at a private university, wearing a top hat just like his father, two or three more doctors of law with their highly esteemed wives, and the honorable Senator, a member of the central committee of a patriotic political party and owner of a house on Hyperion Balenteković Street, who was also, in his turn, opposed to motor transport.

Director-General Domaćinski, the host, naturally played the leading role that pleasant September evening, mild and soft as glycerine, in an unusually green moonlight. He was chairman of an industrial cartel where I was secretary-general and legal adviser, the manufacturer of tin buckets and chamber pots that he had recently exported in large quantities to Persia; a self-made man who had been a waiter, a smuggler, a wartime supplier, a banker, a landlord, a shipowner, a member of a golf-club board; a naive person using what he thought of as highly important and mysterious words like "occasion," "chauffeur," "Little Entente," or "treasury" as self-confidently as if it were all as clear as two and two making four. Well, in this way the Director-General delivered one of his famous monologues, carefully listened to by his obedient servants on all the industrial, commercial, technical, and other boards and at dinner parties with all professional, executive, and managerial officers.

As on similar occasions, next to the Director-General were seated financially weaker and subordinate persons: *homo cylindriacus, vir doctus,* together with his son, the fiancé-to-be of the only daughter of the Director-General, Miss Renata Domaćinski. The Senator, who was also the manufacturer of patent nails, a by-product of tin chamber pots, was subordinate to the Director-General, as were other honorable lawyers and legal advisers, dentists and gynecologists attending the clients of the Director-General; and, finally, among the guests at the dinner party in the vineyard were myself, with my wife Agnes and her baritone as a triangle of hangers-on to this illustrious group. Roast suckling pig, as the first dish, and mocha tart, thick as mud on All Saints' Day, as the dessert, were served in the vineyard under the milky lights surrounded by moths. Hot coffee was also served in silver coffee pots, and in glittering glassware the famous wine called Riesling from the vineyard of Director-General Domaćinski, a professional innkeeper, bartender, and vintner.

The Director-General multiplies two by two, which logically makes four, of course, and four divided by two, of course, is two; on the other hand, by subtracting two from two, of course, nothing is left and the capital, of course, bears dividends, and the dividends, of course, in turn, compel the main capital to make increasing profit, as is perfectly clear. This is how people fight for the markets and evidently this is how it comes to a boom, of course. As for the Jews, they should of course be boycotted, as they do not rank within the spheres of interest of the Director-General, who is booming as a dealer in chamber pots exported to Persia; and moreover they do not of course belong to our group, and things on our planet should of course be settled, both energetically and logically, as it is necessary to rule today by resorting to a gun, a Browning, and the gallows, of course. Praise be to God, wisdom has proved triumphant. The world is no longer so stupid as to be made a fool of by some revolutionaries.

The Director-General, as a chief and employer, was a real pedantic nag and, with his elementary-school cultural background, for many years now had been boring people, but his signature was worth all that vexation. This dullard, obsessed by his own words that rattle like something on an empty table, hears nobody and nothing except his own voice, and is enamored of his own dignity. He thinks of his own knowledge and wisdom in the superlative and thus lectures the boards, the rectors, the universities, the press, charitable societies, delegations, political parties, painters, and public opinion. In brief, he, the Director-General, can teach a whole society, since he has been there, he has seen it, he has heard everything, he has been told something at the most authoritative administrative level, he has been awarded decorations, a memorial plate has been put up for him and a plaque engraved, he has done a lot of traveling, has seen many things with his own eyes, has been convinced that this is so and so and will remain as such, i.e., that might makes right and that greater strength results in more authority. When, one or two years ago, a strike broke out at his factory of chamber pots intended for Persia, he displayed an amazing genius. He did not let any-body dupe him by labor-union intrigues and, when other people wanted to explain to him how his workers had been suffering, he was amazed how other people could not see the situation clearly: he was a little better off in this business because he was just one person and, as for the workers, my God, there was such a multitude of them! It would have been regrettable if business could not secure prosperity at least for one man. He knew how those things had been resolutely solved in Frankfurt, in Nuremberg, in Salamanca; he had read Rosenberg; he knew what the colonial riffraff was, and, as for our peasants, they were only good enough to work at other people's orders and not to be managers. He knew the plans of the Quai d'Or-say and that was why, if you please, in 1918, when in this same vineyard, from this very veranda, he himself shot the four bandits, the four men, rebels and green coats, the revolutionary pigs, he knew as early as that what trend Europe was going to take in its further development. In effect, everything was logical and clear enough, as required by the interests of European public opinion, the interests of European morals and dignity, the interests of a healthy nation full of vitality.

Taking it all in all, everything was perfectly clear and logical: for a full thirty years I had been listening to a whole gang of such directors-general telling everybody how they had been there, how they had witnessed everything with their own eyes, how such and such had been confirmed to them by the highest authorities in the administration, how everything they had been creating, selling, buying, earning, and shooting was in the interests of a healthy nation. And to tell the truth, never until that fateful September night illuminated by the green fragrant moonlight that was so starry and warm had it ever occurred to me to see things objectively, to observe from a distance such a speaker, to separate oneself from one's own gray mask and drift down one's own stream. The secret of my own passivity could be explained in terms of my foolish, unpleasant profession. To act as a lawyer dealing with banks, chamber pots, balance sheets, promissory notes, having to defend absolutely pointless things and relations that are incompatible with higher standards brings about, in the end, a loss of the sense of reality; the feelings are dulled, both the individual and other people are dulled and turned into top-hatted people as well as dullards; one becomes the son-in-law of a druggist and is made a cuckold by a baritone; one has a feeling of being an inferior good-for-nothing, and this is how one disappears like a shadow in a vacuum. This is how, in a unique and dramatic moment, the shadow was turned into a man who began to talk. And that was all. . . .

Afterwards, when the "event" was being retold and assuming the dimensions of a scandal, it was rumored in the town that I had reached in my pocket for a Browning, that even on my arrival in the vineyard, where I was late in coming, I had been very excited, and that in the drawing room a tense scene had taken place between my-

self and the baritone. The rumor was that I had interrupted Domaćinski in his speech and dropped a glass from my hand because, even
before the dinner, I had been very excited, visibly absent-minded,
distressed, hysterical. But this was not really true. Just the opposite:
I was uncommonly calm, composed, and fully aware of everything,
down to the minutest detail. I clearly remember that the stupid
apocalyptic mask of a swollen old drunkard with a gold pince-nez,
bushy mustache, and thick eyebrows had really seemed to me a dull
and empty thing. I had the impression of looking at something me-
chanical, wound up, timed; something not alive but made up so as
to move and speak as a ghostly doll, something impersonal—a
model of a man and not a live human being. And so this impression—that this was not a living man but a wooden doll—excluded
every possibility of any special unrest, and caused even less excite-
ment on my part. Confronted by a doll in a box, one feels like a
superman.

As I remember, that night I could calmly master the situation. I
was seated on the veranda in the vineyard, in the drunken society of
our doctors' elite, I myself a doctor among doctors, rectors, deans,
lecturers, veterinary surgeons, gynecologists, directors-general, their
wives, my wife, a lawyer among lawyers, legal adviser of an industrial trust, a landlord among landlords, a mask among masks, myself
slightly European among Europeans. Sitting there after an abundant
dinner, drinking coffee and sipping the wine (I had not drunk even
two glasses of it), I was listening to the Director-General talking
to the ladies, to his wife, to my wife, to his daughter, whose suitor
and fiancé-to-be sat worriedly next to her, absolutely at a loss as
to his risky expectations, and to my elder daughter Agnes, seated
next to her mother and the baritone. He was talking about late
autumn in 1918 when here, in our country, the green coats were
devastating these regions and when the Director-General had shot

four bandits one after another, like hares, firing from a military carbine: two near the pillar next to the cellar, another a little farther away, near an arbor, and one farther down, at the far end of the vineyard, while he was trying to jump over a fence. They planned to break into the cellar of the Director-General but he shot them: two were instantly shot in the head on the spot, the one near the vine arbor got two bullets in his left lung, and the last one, who fell near the fence, bled to death after the artery in his neck had been hit.

Surrounded by ladies, gentlemen, and citizens, I rested my right hand on the table while slowly turning with my index finger and thumb the eight-sided stem of a crystal glass: the wine glittered splendidly in the antiquated gaslight; the perfectly round milky light was mirrored in the shining wine, the moonlight was green, the crickets could be heard from the vineyard, and Director-General Domaćinski was telling a gay anecdote of how, in 1918, he had shot four men there like four dogs, at several steps' distance from the veranda. The Director-General is a banker, a wine wholesaler, a vintner, the proprietor of sawmills, and a distinguished businessman. He is one of ours, has his own "chauffeur," his "portraits," his "Quai d'Orsay." Incidentally, he had a new main altar built in the baroque parish church below the vineyard, which by moonlight looks like a white patch in the distance. On his orders, as the donor, the two main stained-glass windows were colorfully painted, showing motifs cherished by the Director-General: an angel lamenting at Christ's empty tomb, and Christ on the River Jordan. The windows were marked in stylized Gothic letters: "Donated by A. Domaćinski in his own name and in that of his wife Helena." And who could have possibly explained to that donor that he was obviously and logically nobody else but one of the commonest and most vulgar of criminals, a murderer; morally an idiot, a criminal type of man? Who could have explained to that uncultured ignoble man that he was a commonplace criminal and assassin, not for having killed and slain, not because he had caused the four mad dogs to bleed, as he put it, but because this evening he was telling a story about it as a praiseworthy adventure he had experienced in 1918, at a time when he, as a prophet and "farsighted politician," eighteen years ago knew and foretold the turn European policy was to take in its development? If one even managed to explain to that type of man that in man's life there were also other categories besides that of rifleman, all the insane people at this table covered with a white damask tablecloth under the opaque lights would think such a man was drunk, confused and certainly naive. If, according to logic, one were to prove that he had not been drunk but only had a logical mind, if one were to expound the theme that our peasants, "the rebellious swine of outlaws," were in reality no bandits, but that at the time the walls of a prison had been breaking apart after a centuries-long unjust state of affairs, that it was a question of a genuine international catastrophe, of an elementary, practically primeval disaster, and that our peasants were by no means mad dogs in those days but, on the contrary, people who were rising from the indignity of humiliated slaves, the gentlemen around the table would not have understood it, they would have been unable to grasp such a thing because, in effect, the gentlemen around the table lacked even the most elementary prerequisites to comprehend such logical thinking.

The "mad dogs" wanted to rob his cellar, to empty his costly barrels of wine, and he fired at them to defend his wine, which was undoubtedly his own property. However, when the other "mad dogs" —the emperor's and king's dogs—bottled and poured that same wine of his within the framework of requisition—and even other people's blood, which was likewise somebody's property—he did not, of course, fire at representatives of the imperial and royal au-

thorities, since it was lawful requisition of the wine, in compliance
with the laws concerned. At that time, the Director-General did not,
of course, fight on the battlefield, but made money as a meat- and
fat- and brandy-supplier amid the massacre that was not, by any
means, any kind of "criminal massacre" but a "just war," exclusively
conducted for that purpose, i.e., that such and similar idiots could
earn money as patriots and decent people. The Director-General did
not open fire to protest against the requisition of his wine in wartime but against "mad dogs" who, barking in general against the
injustice of the war, had begun a struggle against the entire war
machine. And what kind of laws are those that enable the Director-
General to shoot at mad dogs who oppose the war rather than at
those who requisition his wine and wish to carry war further? It is
all a crime, a bloody thing, moral insanity.

At the table, with head bent, holding the polished glass stem in
my right hand, absorbed in thought, completely calm, without any
undertone betraying irritation, more to myself than anybody else, I
absent-mindedly said that "it was all a crime, a bloody thing, moral
insanity."

By pure chance, this naive phrase in my soliloquy coincided with
a pause between two sentences uttered by the Director-General—
dead silence. And because of that dead silence, special significance
was attached to every individual word I said. Thereupon it was rumored in the town that, infuriated, almost mad, I had yelled at the
top of my lungs, that I had jumped and pulled the tablecloth, shouting at those present and denouncing them as moral idiots, and that
angrily I had even stuck out my tongue at them and dashed into
the vineyard like a werewolf. It was all untrue. Absorbed in my
thought, I remarked in a very low voice, rather sentimentally and
with a suppressed sigh—as if talking to myself—that it was all morally insane, that it would be nonsensical to discuss anything with

such foolish people who have never known how, nor wanted to either, to think along the lines of any logic that does not bring about some kind of profit. If, at that moment, my statement could have any deeper meaning at all, then it was only what it really was: a gesture suggesting that there was no sense in wasting time in futile talks with people who were not even human beings.

But just the opposite occurred. Those last banal, trite phrases, suggesting how everything was morally corroded, exploded at that table on the veranda like a rocket in a cloud of smoke over the silverware and lamps and masks.

The Director-General—his belly protruding, with pouting lips, with horizontal wrinkles on his low stiff forehead, and with a burning match in his right hand—watched everything from under his pince-nez while lighting his third Havana. He then stopped for a while to inhale through his cigar and, holding it half lit in his hand between the left index and the middle finger, leaned toward me and, expressing sudden surprise as if wondering what I had in mind, asked me what was bloody and what crime was in question.

"Everything: your wine, the four dead men you described as mad dogs. You see, you've been telling us about this all evening. Well, that's it. . . ."

"How do you mean? I don't get you," said the Director-General, still expecting me to explain what I had muttered from behind my teeth so as to enable him to breathe two or three times at peace through his Havana before the match was extinguished in his hand.

"How do you mean—morally insane? What crime? What is bloody about it?"

"Well, you have been telling us about it, boasting of having shot four men. Anybody can shoot a man if the opportunity arises. But only individual persons prone to crime can boast of murder. That is what I mean by a morally insane situation."

"Then you approve of the burglary? If that's so, I regret not having shot you too, as the fifth."

He was drunk, talking like that amid a cloud of smoke, arrogantly self-assured as a non-commissioned officer yelling at recruits. A moth could be heard desperately fluttering its wings inside a milky glass lamp. Then a fairly long pause followed. I can still visualize the oil lamp looking strange and unusually opaque above the bowls containing fruit and cakes. It was like the smeared reflection of the light of an antiquated hearse. Everybody at the table was gazing at me, wondering why I was still silent. It seemed to me as if I were in the theater, on the stage, acting, and that it was my turn to speak: unless I began to speak, the whole performance would come to a halt, the theater would go bankrupt, the curtain would fall in the middle of a scene.

I was still immobile at the table, with my right hand feeling the polished sharp edges of the glass stem between my two fingers. I also remembered how, between my thumb and index finger, my heart pulsated. Its beat was echoed in the eight-sided glass stem, regularly, monotonously: one, two, three, four, five, six, seven. . . . It was still my turn to speak. The faces around the table were stiff, as if they were being photographed by a clumsy beginner in photography who never appeared from beneath the black cloth while we waited for his apparatus to click so that life could continue to murmur in wine-drinking, amid stupidity, laughter, moonlight, to fly like the moth that, after a fearful struggle, soared out of the milky lamp and disappeared beyond the vault of the veranda, high above our heads, into the green distances of a warm September night.

My composure at the time is evident from my still-vivid memories of every detail, even the most trifling. So the subsequent rumors in the town about my grimaces, yelling, and profound, rather abnormal, feverish restlessness were completely unfounded. I was calm and almost like a visionary, fully aware of the far-reaching effects of every one of my words and movements. I still saw a possibility of the so-called conventional denouement, as did every trained dog barking at his master inside the room: putting its tail between its legs and taking shelter under the table from the kick or the whip. A thousand open opportunities, a rich variety of possibilities, began to dawn upon me. I could have concentrated on some general considerations about the term "moral insanity," saying nothing and recognizing the Director-General as a genial and visionary politician since, as far back as 1918, he knew that one should shoot people like "mad dogs" . . . Yet, having uttered the concluding sentence of my intimate soliloquy without any ulterior motive, without the least malicious or aggressive intention in mind as that conclusion had emerged logically and, by pure coincidence, fluttered above the heads of the dullards on the veranda, and feeling fascinated by the naiveté of my little truth, I realized that I could not do this by any means: putting my tail between my legs at that moment would have amounted to disappearing under the table like a dog at the time when, after fifty years, I had first said openly what seemed, according to human logic, natural to me.

Gold bridges, porcelain teeth, the red faces from under the eyeglasses and pince-nez, the warm smell of female flesh, the extremely stupid goggling eyes of my distinguished wife, Domaćinski's Havana, the raised arms of the Magnificus exclaiming, "But, Doctor!" . . . Perhaps the dignified appeal by that Magnificus to my doctor's dignity, to the lofty bourgeois position of my academic profession, separated me even more from that half-drunk group of people. And so I let go the stem of my glass and put my hand into my pocket to get my cigarette case. I do not know how Domaćinski interpreted this gesture, but he seemed to me to grab a bottle because of his

crazy notion that I wanted to shoot him. By that time we were surrounded by the gentlemen from among the guests. Amid a great
commotion, shouts that it was all meaningless, that the gentlemen
should calm down, that everything was a misunderstanding. I heard
Domaćinski's hoarse bass asking me unconditionally and impera-
tively to take back my words, to give him satisfaction, and to apologize because, otherwise, he would shoot me like a dog.

I lit a cigarette and rose to my feet.

To whom should I apologize? For what? I stated that the gentleman had been boasting of having shot four men like four dogs, I
stuck to my story: it was all criminal and morally insane. I did not
at all intend to apologize, especially not to a bandit threatening to
kill me too. And only the fact that I was a guest in his house prevented me from treating his new criminal outbreak as would have
been only logical.

I remember no further detail. Everybody was shouting; above all
thundered the bass of our host Domaćinski yelling that he would
shoot me like a dog. Robust and fleshy, he broke away from the
crowd of doctors and senators and, howling like a madman that he
would not permit anyone to insult him in his own house, that he
would himself take satisfaction, and that he would trample me
down on the spot, he attacked me. As soon as I noticed a revolver
glittering in his hand, I overturned the table, jumped over all the
bowls, lamps, and glassware, and disappeared into the night. I
heard the clinking of the glassware, the tableware, the lamps, along
with frightful yelling and screaming on the veranda wrapped in the
twilight. And outside, in the night, the wind rattling in the chestnuts, the crickets, the moonlight, and the dewy, green, starry silence.
The wind in the branches, the singing crickets, the stars . . .

3

THE STORM
OVER THE SMALL TOWN

In our small backwater, the event in the vineyard took on scandalous proportions. A witch hunt began, putting me overnight into
complete isolation in the middle of a wasp's nest of prejudice and
mindless folly. Everything started as stupidly as Carl Maria von
Weber's "Invitation to a Waltz," the favorite piece of music of my
wife, a druggist's daughter called Agnes.

R. M. Floriani, an old-fashioned bon vivant, had a typically fleshy
eighteenth-century double chin, was a refined man, carefully and
even more than pedantically dressed, polished, with gloves in his
left hand. At first sight he appeared to be perfectly balanced (until

you discovered bracelets under his cuffs), a gentleman who, with utmost attention, offered everyone he talked to a cigarette from a costly golden case bearing his monogram. And that irreproachable gentleman who made it a practice to be the first to greet his acquaintances, not only because he was so well brought up and so well-dressed but also because, above all, he was convinced that modesty was the most outstanding attribute of all genuine refinement—that gentleman who was balanced in every respect, leaning slightly to the right and hardly noticeably dragging his right sole on the pavement, a man walking at a measured gait in all his tastes, convictions, and passions—a gentleman who, as the most polite person in our town, never had an affair or conflict with anyone, was among the first to refuse to greet me. In the club, while playing poker, he demonstratively declared aloud his full agreement with Domaćinski, adding that I should really be shot like a "mad dog." . . .

That I should be shot like a mad dog came to be the favorite slogan broadcast and popularized by the Sarvašes. The Sarvašes have been high officials for three generations. The forebears of that blue-blooded clan were legal representatives of motor car and typewriter manufacturing firms, Rotarians and Masons. For several years I had, by sheer accident, been involved in an intricate inheritance dispute with the Sarvaš clan, my wife's relatives. Frankly, I never approached those gentlemen with an open heart or sympathy. I knew that family of impostors well, according to what my wife said about them, and she was their cousin. And, having been acquainted with the behind-the-scenes truth about those miserably obsessed people who, as judges, judged other people according to their own interests, and as lawyers regarded everybody as natural-born victims, I never liked those lackeys serving other people's interests, always ready to do service to anybody who could pay them well; those imperial counselors decorated with the highest orders; those stingy landlords constantly involved in lawsuits with their tenants. What I say about them was true, and they took full revenge on me, as is only logical, after all. Under absolutism, one member of the Sarvaš family was the Emperor's informer, and that national shame, translated into imperial and royal titles, was interpreted as the glamourous tradition of the Sarvaš-Daljski family. One of the younger members of that noble family, Egon von Sarvaš, was a most disorderly and frivolous lover whose three divorce cases in two years I had conducted. He was a lascivious man by nature who did not experience a minute of calm in his unutterably complicated life of exciting love affairs and their consequences. That haughty and idiotic representative of our so-called gentry, who dealt in sales of bandage material, was actually some sort of procurer, supplying both his male and female protectors with female and male services, and he was the first to break the news of "the Strindbergian hell of my married life." It was from him, or rather through him, that I learned my wife Agnes had been "one of the unhappiest wives on earth" and that for years "her sole ideal had been to get rid of my oppression, of my excessive drinking, and of my lascivious life."

It sounds bizarre, but that does not make it less true. Within those few dramatic days I heard more about my wife Agnes than I could have seen with my own eyes during my whole tedious marriage to her. Before the scandal with Domaćinski, I did not have the slightest idea that I was more intensely hated and despised by her than by anyone else on earth.

Amalia Aquacurti-Sarvaš-Daljski, the widow of the Austrian General Aquacurti, all of whose grandfathers and great-grandfathers had died in asylums showing signs of megalomania and pretending to have been emperors, popes, or admirals—that old, toothless, insane scarecrow picked up the thesis launched by her talented grandson Egon von Sarvaš-Daljski and, from that provincial postal system, spread the rumor that I had infected my wife with a venereal disease, had had an unhappy marriage for many years, was overstrained, almost insane, in debt, unaccountable; in brief: crazy—ready for an asylum, of course not as an admiral or pope or emperor, but as a commonplace idiot.

That is how the whole affair began to evolve during a poker party at old R. M. Floriani's; that is how the news was magnified by my wife's cousin Egon von Sarvaš-Daljski and then expertly elaborated and supplied with various convincing proofs by the aged Amalia. From the old Aquacurti's house the rumor was spread through the town by the women of the Čungos family, the Damaskinis and the Dagmar Varagonskis, who behaved like regular magpies, parrots, and chatterboxes. The news was spread further by the wives of the Domaćinskis and the Balentekovićs, the wives of the rectors, directors, doctors, lecturers, and finally by the women of the Čupek household and the Gumbeks. At last all this news became a flood: I had reached for a revolver; at the very last moment I had been prevented from shooting all the guests; I had demolished the whole villa; I had caught my wife in the very act of adultery; she had caught me in the very act of adultery; my blood test had been positive; I was prone to an anarchist outlook on life; my house had been searched; I had been in a straitjacket; and so on and so forth. . . .

Everybody was as alarmed as if plague had broken out. Tedious gray faces, dusty and suspicious people fishing in troubled waters who, when filling out questionnaires during political inquiries declare in public over their own signatures that they have no concern with politics, began to whisper and murmur in cafés about me as "a politically dangerous person who should be expelled from bourgeois society in the interests of political morals, since he preaches destructive, anarchistic principles of individual action." These beggars, intellectual good-for-nothings, blueblooded fools, the ones imagining themselves to be the descendants of imaginary pretenders to imaginary thrones, scribblers abounding in unhealthy ambitions, imitators of other people's stupidities, dignitaries, orators, lecturers, insane people who chew on their own sorry careers as if they were pralines, all those ridiculous little thieves who would lick anybody's boots for a ladyfinger, the pillars of a society built on curettage, representatives of a science dictated from above on administrative orders—this whole rabble had been fed in my house over the years, stealing my cigarettes, eating whole dishes of fish and game. Those insignificant merchants dealing in horseshoes and patent nails, stout chief clerks in Domaćinski's banks who had married rich butchers' daughters from backward provinces, the old women, pudgy, fleshy, red in the face, swollen as if after scarlet fever, loaded down with gold brooches and bracelets—everybody poked his nose into the lies and slanders and began hissing and whispering to one another that poor Agnes's husband, the son-in-law of the druggist, the famous inventor of a tea for digestion, and the owner of a three-storied house with a balcony on the main street, had gone mad and wanted to shoot Director-General Domaćinski but was prevented from doing it, and that the whole affair would be settled in court.

Jewelers, dentists, better-off salesmen, technical section chiefs, Romance linguists, cellists, shoe dealers, freethinkers, Lamarckians, pediatricians, wholesalers and private employees, cosmeticians and specialists in skin diseases, barons, landlords, master tailors who tailor books with their pens on schedule and according to measure, hired agitators talking against their own convictions, social nobodies who collect contributions for illegitimate children just as they babble about the dangers of air raids on unprotected cities, bankrupt bankers, state finance administrators, signatories to political proclamations they themselves do not believe in, liars who swear in public to convictions they despise, smugglers, the press, drunkards, nonsmokers, old maids—everything and everybody grew as agitated as sparrows on St. Valentine's Day. Everyone, according to the logic of his digestion, intestines, and warm blankets, started to growl, to bark, to slander, to gossip, to find out, to deal with the case of Domaćinski's chief lawyer, the son-in-law of a druggist, the proprietor of a house with a balcony situated at the corner of the street near the bishop's memorial.

From my earliest childhood I have suffered an unusually intense fear when seeing wax statues. The painted imitation of human heads or hands in waxlike objects sold at fairs causes an inexplicable nervous spasm in my stomach. As a beginning high school student, I used to get terrible diarrhea from visually repulsive experiences. Why, for instance, don't the sides of beef or the slaughtered hogs in butcher-shop windows make us vomit or upset our intestines? The bleeding, sore patches of animal meat provide unquestionable proof of a revolting, base murder, but a genuinely carnivorous animal considers fat and bleeding hogs cut in two most appealing since, above all, they can be used as food. But the wax mold of a cross section of the kidneys, the intestines, the digestive or sexual tracts has a sickening effect. It suggests the meaninglessness and pointlessness of life. It has a melancholy effect on man's mind, I cannot help feeling, only because in it life is objectivized to a degree bordering on disgust. That life, in a backwater like our town, was in reality as senseless as one of these wax molds at fairs was something I usually dismissed. But I could dismiss it no longer. Everything was corroded in front of me like a wax mold of female genitals attacked by cancer, cut in two for exhibition, so that I myself, a fifty-year-old insane man who had wasted his whole life on futile hospitality offered to dullards, began to react with sheer disgust to it all.

True, even earlier I suspected how it was with people. I knew that public statisticians, those distinguished scientists who publish thick books of facts—which no one reads or takes seriously—embellish their facts, since it is an international custom to believe that the world is better if the number of lavatories, canals, shipbuilding, rails, rifles and machines in general are on the increase. With such gentlemen and distinguished chiefs of our statistics I could carouse, drink to mutual friendship and brotherhood, play chess, talk about the question of the Far East. But the problem was: What attitude should you take toward a statistician who wants to classify you, among his columns, under the category of the punished? That you can rewrite history according to your own needs, "along the lines of opportunity," as they say, was known to me. Or that you can buy a medical certificate from a physician, or a book review from a critic, love from a woman, a higher rank at a good dinner and, generally, promotion, I knew all too well. In that kind of transaction I myself have taken part to some extent. For treating people like the wounded, or like miserable dwarfs, I had my own method, i.e., compassion and sympathy for the wretches who did not have any common sense of their own and could not, consequently, be expected to possess either morals or will and who therefore were not to blame for being part of the stale mixture of universal illiteracy and paralysis that is our domestic situation.

Thus, I was sorry for my fellow countrymen and my judgment was: you paint without taste; as self-taught artists, you do not really know how to paint; you have no particular talent; I therefore buy your bad paintings against my own conviction because nobody else wants to buy your paintings, your exhibitions have no visitors and smell of a mortuary. Everything, both the laurel in the flowerpots and the tired footsteps of a passer-by who has lost his way, looks sad, as if a dead body were lying somewhere behind the screen. Or: you write books, you are disorganized, superficial, rather stupid; you know absolutely nothing about anything, the first signs of the exhaustion of old age are already visible, but you are still playing the role of a local dignitary; you talk about worthless ideas, yell, do not trust even your own self, spread confusion and, in self-defense, deceive the people around you. And why? Nobody buys your books, and if some naive person happens to leaf through that wonderful artichoke of yours, he gets a headache. In your turn, you get a headache from a printed review of your book, and the question is why and what for?

The deceitful pathos of lies. The god in the churches is as lifeless as the saints on the altars, and so every single word we hear from the pulpit is uninspired: a poorly paid service, and the clacking of artificial teeth. In reality, everything taking place around, in front of, or against the church is equally lifeless and uninspired. Modern friars, on the basis of their new outlook on life, deny the right to existence to friars with feudal ideas. To discuss God with contemporary infidels is by no means less tedious than to permit the faithful in Franciscan robes with medieval ideas to bore you. Incidentally, it is far more complicated to be an infidel than to be a friar who spits three times at the mention of Luther's name. In hospitals, around operating tables, distinguished butchers in their white uniforms are as conceited as actresses in the theater: the notion of success in life is to them more important than anything else. Generally, everything in life is a matter of success, and success in itself signifies sleeping: a pleasant sleep with hot and cold running water, a sleep without a toothache or any special soporifics, a calm, sound sleep when consciousness is at rest, when the brain is not at work, when one travels in a sleeping car and smokes the finest tobacco. Success is an end in itself, and success is for the sake of success, and everything is for the sake of success: big and trifling lies, dinners and tea parties, circles of people, friendships, deceptions, hatreds, wars, and careers. To secure success, roles are being played, masks worn; everybody is afraid of failure. Ideas are confused, and success is the only criterion: you kill people; you wear elegant, pointed shoes, well-ironed trousers; you put polish on your nails; you travel; you deal in trade; you have houses built; you conduct wars; you write books; you make paintings; you are on a lighted stage, in an office, on a newspaper editorial board, and you do not realize that life is not really what it is thought to be in offices, on the stage, or in the press.

And this is where lies the key to understanding my situation in this backwater town of ours after the so-called event in the vineyard of Director-General Domaćinski: by that time I had been watching from a distance the masked ball that murmured down below in the street under my first-floor balcony, although I was not actually aware that I was personally nothing but an ordinary mask in the short-sighted folly that was brewing. However, as soon as I became aware of this, the situation changed: instead of being a silent man who was only a passive onlooker, I was transformed into another person who had stopped acting after realizing how false his whole acting had been, how insincere, as they say of actors on the real stage. So I stopped playing the role of a Samaritan, a compassionate person exclusively preoccupied with other people's cares, and very shortly I realized that life under the new conditions was far more complicated for me than it had seemed at first. Over the thirty years of my more-or-less successful acting and pretending, people created an image of me as a silent man, passive, good-humored (meaning rather stupid), a Ph.D. who could invite them to dinner, buy their pictures or sign a promissory note. But that that same impersonal individual could have his own opinion, especially an opinion differing from their own, was beyond the capacity of their fancy. They were unexpectedly confused thereby, and it could account for their at-first-sight incomprehensible and, in the main, general agree-

ment that I was suffering some sort of derangement of my brain.
Certainly, since I had stopped thinking along the lines of their logic,
I might very well have seemed mad. Their "logic" was a kind of
conventional social game played according to fixed rules. The rules
read: the world is as it is, and it should not be improved. The game
of dominoes is played to win, and everything else is sheer "philoso-
phizing." . . . Being self-denyingly conventional, I had never phi-
losophized, *pro foro externo,* and this was to my disadvantage later
on. I pitied people, I was politely inclined toward them. Since I
knew them thoroughly under their own skins and since I felt sorry
for them for being so helplessly gray, so insensitively dull, so miserable and such cheap playthings in other people's hands, so fatally
disfigured by their own folly, I was naturally able to share their
cares, lose time on their lawsuits, pity those quasi-talents in our
midst while watching how they lived in humid rooms, starving
in foggy weather, devoid of any special ability except for clay-
modeling or writing two or three lines of rhymed verse. When that
army of small sparrow-mouthed scavengers was disturbed over my
"pathological" case, when those merchants dealing in delicacies,
stockbrokers, retired assistant professors, untalented painters, poets,
all those short-sighted ignoramuses, according to the laws of their
hare-brained natures, revolted against me as "a morally insane person," when they began snubbing me with indignation while passing
on to their own follies, I stopped pretending to be a good-natured
silent man and began to behave sincerely. I turned my back on them
without any comment in response to their impudence, saying nothing but good-by.

What should I have said to such intellectual harpies, such imaginary greatnesses portraying goldfish or writing poems about apples
on a plate, when they approached me and tapped me on the shoul-

der and suggested that they could not see why I should have been so irritated over it all, suggesting my nerves must be frayed and that I best go abroad to recuperate.

Where did I fray my nerves? When? Where am I going to take a rest abroad? Why? Because I told a Domaćinski that he was a criminal type of man? Well, he really is a criminal type. I'm sorry but, after everything that has happened, that is what I think of him.

Among the petit-bourgeois fools around me incredible confusion arose. The doctors, landlords, café habitués, internists, people creeping one on top of the other, people being screwed into each other, people fattening like tapeworms on other people's intestines, descendants of umbrella manufacturers and musicians, titled dullards living in the shadow of great reputations, astronomers stealing texts from their colleagues, cocaine smugglers, forgers of workers' insurance certificates, brick-kiln workers, window dressers, retired military court judges—one and all they became alarmed at the very thought of the existence of one individual flying his own flag.

Ex-Minister Pankracije Harambašević, a gentleman with sideburns, bought himself several two-storied houses by the most incredibly fantastic issues of diverse series of stamps while he was still in office. That professional elementary-school geometry teacher, who, as a minister, pushed his way to the position of a delegate to the League of Nations and now plays chess in one of the distinguished cafés at the other end of the row of trees in the city center, felt it behooved him to express his deep personal dissatisfaction with my misbehavior toward Director-General Domaćinski.

Did I have any notion of the role played by that excellent man in the development of "our young economy?" Our liqueurs, our coal, our lumber, our textiles, our press—everything—was the personal achievement of Domaćinski. Anybody denying his role of pioneer in the building of our economy was nothing but impertinent. And since his role was not at all unknown to me, for me to say such a thing was in fact incomprehensible. . . .

"And what is, by the way, incomprehensible?"

"How do you mean, what is incomprehensible? Well, dear Doctor, I beg your pardon, you are not going to deny that . . ."

"What? What have I been denying? Even if I denied something, what could that have to do with our liqueurs, or with our fabrics, which, since they are not mine, cannot be 'ours,' either. They are perhaps yours. . . ."

"I beg your pardon, Doctor. . . . Oh, I . . . nothing. You know, you are a professional lawyer, you must know better than I what is opportune: to deny it or not?"

"That's perfectly logical, Minister. I am a lawyer, I am not a philatelist. I am neither a landlord nor a minister. . . ."

"You ought to be sent to a clinic for examination. You are unaware of the far-reaching consequences of your speech. What tasteless allusions are these? I don't understand it. I beg your pardon. . . ."

"I repeat, Minister, I'm completely unfamiliar with postage stamps: I've never been a postal clerk, I've never dealt in stamps. I'm a lawyer, I pay stamp duty; I don't issue stamps in order to build houses. Good-by."

In a whole series of these perfectly superfluous encounters in the street, I remained consistent, simply following the line of common sense, without any determined ulterior motive. And when I threw young Von Petretich into the pool under the waterfall, it was not in any fit of madness but an explicable human gesture, more in moral than physical self-defense. A sniveler, a silly self-styled provincial patrician whose father had always lived in the grand style, a young

man brought up in an environment where people behave like the
shabbiest salesmen—which is to say they are humble prior to the
expiration of a promissory note and incredibly arrogant as soon as
they have something to jingle in their pockets—this Von Petretich,
ex-cavalry officer, approached me in the park while I was watching
the goldfish in the pool below the waterfall playing in the shade of
a white waterlily, the tiny silvery bubbles of oxygen rising vertically
to the glassy surface of the water around the green flat leaves. He
approached me from the back and I remember it clearly—he
neither shook hands with me nor raised his hat. With his right hand
on the silvery surface of his cigarette case, against which he was
tapping his cigarette, that impostor, my junior by at least fifteen
years, stopped and, after resting his right foot on the stone edge of
the pool, he smiled ironically or, rather, provocatively at me like a
man intending to provoke a conflict at all costs.

"You are, my dear Doctor, staring at the water as if you were
contemplating suicide."

"No, I've been observing these tiny goldfish. Fish are not particularly intelligent. I don't know whether you've ever watched
them in an aquarium. They don't know the difference between
glass and water. They swim in one direction until they sense
through the mouth the impossibility of swimming any farther
through the glass, but they completely dismiss that experience once
they turn to the other end of the aquarium. Their stupidity has been
in existence for eternity . . ."

"And I thought you were planning to drown yourself! I heard
that Domaćinski is going to challenge you to a duel. Ha-ha."

"To a duel? Me? Domaćinski?"

"Are you scared? A petty merchant like Domaćinski—such a
keg-tapper never challenged anyone to a duel. Don't be afraid, Doc-

tor. Had you told me to my face all that you said to that old par-
venu, I would have made you bleed by lashing you like a dog. But
Domaćinski is not, of course, going to do anything about it."

"And you would not do me the honor to challenge me to a duel?
Please, tell me why?"

"It would be humiliating for me. Insane people like you deserve
to be whipped like dogs. You are not worthy of satisfaction. You
are a Communard."

What should I have answered such a fool, who had been occupy-
ing various posts for some ten or fifteen years but could not prove
in any other way except by the thick skin of his rear end that he
had done a lick of work? He had heard Oscar Strauss's *Waltz
Dream* twenty-two times; otherwise a vacuum prevailed within
him. I slapped him in the face so vigorously that he fell down, join-
ing the small goldfish, and everything ended in a big rush of children, governesses, and policemen. It was a strange experience: to find
oneself escorted by a policeman into a cab with a man whose cloth-
ing was dripping wet and who twice spat in my face. He would have
attacked me but he had a fracture of his left wrist, and two policemen were holding him, convinced that he was an irresponsible luna-
tic. From time to time he screamed with pain so infuriatingly that
I myself was under the impression he was mad. A whole crowd of
children and servants rushed behind us and then, at the police station, everything was cleared up. We left the building separately:
first he, and a few minutes later I, each in his own taxi.

The next day he sent his witnesses to see me. They were Bo-
kanovski and Faltonini: the former was a representative of some
American sewing-machine factory, and as for the latter, within less
than six months he was arrested on espionage charges and I met
him afterward while in confinement awaiting trial. There was a
moving scene between the witnesses and me. I threw them all out.

Three days later a certain Von Floden-Foncière Italo, a similar type of man, brought me the minutes of that event, but I threw him out too, together with the minutes. What idiotic goings-on these were.

"But, my friend, you've been exaggerating," the soap-factory owner, Mr. Bachmayer, remarked. "You can't defend an absurd situation. On one occasion you threaten people with your revolver, on another you demolish whole houses, then you throw people into the water and demonstratively turn your back on your well-meaning friends. My friend, things don't work like that. You yourself should think about the consequences of such conduct. It leads to anarchy, to revolution."

What sort of reply should one give to such a well-meaning conservative soap manufacturer? Either withdraw or push on? Should I tell him that it was not I who had reached for a revolver, but Domaćinski? That it was not I who had been boasting about the murder, but, once again, Domaćinski? How I had not been the first to hurt anyone but had only reacted to the impolite behavior of other people? Or that I had not been threatening to whip Petretich like a dog, but that it was just the other way round?

"No, sir, you don't know the facts. You are acting on a mistaken assumption. At present I have no intention whatsoever of wasting time on details, but you have no idea of how things stand."

"For God's sake, how do you mean, I have no idea? You see, your own wife came to see my wife last night, crying. She said she was the most unfortunate woman in the whole town. She also said she could not make out what had been going on, and in her opinion some action should be taken in your own interests. And I think, too, that it would be best if you went to consult a physician and went away for a rest. . . ."

"Good-by."

So it came to a quarrel here and a break there, a word from this man and a message from another, the opinion of this circle, the conviction of that group, advice from one side and a threat from another; that my own wife considered me a madman; that, through my own fault I could no longer work for the cartel; that my father-in-law, the druggist, had declared in public, in a café, in front of strangers, that he repudiated me; that the best thing would be to consult doctors; to make a bargain, to apologize and face the consequences. In brief: the circus grew increasingly mad every day, more and more infuriating, and at times it seemed to me that everything was hovering in the air and that it would be difficult to guess where it would all end. One thing, however, was perfectly clear to me: one should remain logical because logic has never been an unreliable guide. True, I was rather alone, but loneliness is not proof of not being right.

4

GOOD-BY

The third day following the dinner party in the vineyard I sent a letter to the cartel notifying them that I was sick and that the doctors said I would be unable to fulfill my duties for some time. That dry, official letter contained an enclosure, a medical certificate issued by an old friend of mine, a surgeon, that I had appendicitis and that an operation might very well be indicated.

The next day Dr. Marko Javoršek called me up. He was a lawyer, once a Marxist, a Social-Democratic ex-minister in charge of an economic department in the royal government formed on the basis of a platform that could have been anything but Marxist. Ex-Minister

Javoršek was an economic counselor in the enterprises of Director-General Domaćinski as well as one of his personal friends. On the other hand, he was a member of various management councils: at the sawmill and the chamber-pot factory and even at a perfumery and a drugstore under the trademark of a fashionable and coquettish Egyptian goddess. Minister Marko Javoršek who, as a lawyer, signed his name as Mark Antony and enjoyed the reputation of being an excellent public tribune and a very talented orator, paid me a visit in my own flat at five past twelve sharp the next day, a time agreed on in advance, upon the receipt of my letter by the cartel.

"Be at home, then, dear Doctor, at five past twelve. I'll be there."

And, indeed, at five past twelve he was at my house, and by a quarter past twelve the situation was unquestionably clear: he had come at Domaćinski's request to demand full satisfaction from me, and formally, too.

It was to be in writing, noting first that I regretted the insult, and secondly that I withdrew all slanders—everything I had said, in short, which was founded on the facts—because otherwise he would first fire me out of hand and then deliver me to the court authorities. Minister Mark Antony thought that out of mutual interest we could reach a compromise, make a bargain. A formal letter on my part would relieve Domaćinski of the undoubtedly unpleasant duty of handing me over to the court and, on the other hand, it was in my own interest to settle the scandal in a gentlemanly, European fashion, so that I would be given the chance to receive formal notice and the severance pay guaranteed by law, rather than the other way around: to be put on trial and to quit my post under circumstances that undoubtedly had no special advantage to me from a financial point of view.

I asked Minister Mark Antony to be so kind and tell Domaćinski that I did not intend to write any such letter, that I did not dream of asking satisfaction, and, as for the settlement of obligations—that is, court proceedings—I would be at his disposal. I accepted the notice and acknowledged the filing of his suit against me. As for the material side of the matter, it did not interest me.

"I have no intention, Doctor, of giving you any advice, but I assume you are fully aware of the legal implications of this unpleasant event. Nevertheless, as a friend and colleague, you will allow me to tell you that I cannot help being under the impression that you are a bit excited and cannot therefore be as objective as is necessary when making such important decisions. As you know, this is a question of paragraphs two twenty-nine, three hundred, and three hundred and one of the Penal Code. Beyond all doubt, the verdict will be against you. Domaćinski is a prominent figure, he is one of the outstanding representatives of our economy, he is the holder of a whole series of both domestic and international decorations, he is ... well ... somebody. Why should we waste both time and words? The situation in which you find yourself at present is not, of course, at all enviable, but surely it is preferable to decide to follow the path of least resistance and thus end the affair with decency and with the least malice. Of course, I am in an awkward situation but, in imploring you to trust that all my sympathies in this are on your side and however unpleasant it is to me to appear in this role of an intermediary, I nevertheless believe you have no cause whatever to suspect my friendship for you, and for this particular reason it is imperative that you understand that everybody who is impartial agrees with me in evaluating the whole situation. As it appears to me, you are under the influence of your own rhetoric and therefore lack sufficient moral strength to face facts directly and realize that in life it is often both better and simpler to throw a sprat to catch a herring than—as now—to waste time on uncertainties and eventually lose your last chance."

"My dear Mark Antony, there is not one of our seven thousand doctors of law and philosophy who would not give me the same advice. But again I am at a loss as to what to tell you except to give you a statement that I have already had the honor to make: I accept the notice and acknowledge that I will be brought to trial. I stick to every word in my statement, i.e., that Domaćinski is a criminal type of man, a murderer, and a bandit."

"Would you allow me, colleague, to remark that you have gone too far, if I may say so, in rhetoric? You should come down to earth. What do you mean by denouncing somebody as a bandit? Except for verbal injury, it means absolutely nothing."

"After everything that happened over there on the veranda, I consider that man to be a criminal type. I don't understand what you mean by saying, 'come down to earth.' Domaćinski is beyond doubt a moral idiot."

"But, dear friend, you are impractical in terms of positive legalities. What you have been talking about is possibly poetry, but it has nothing to do with facts, with realities. That is not the way in which politics should be conducted. Every single word you have uttered is an increasingly gross insult."

"Well, have you come over here to instruct me, to teach me how 'politics' should be pursued? I have never dealt with politics and childish intentions of this kind are completely remote from me."

"Politics in the figurative sense, my dear colleague, do exist. In life everything amounts to politics and politics serve us as a means for achieving the goal we want to attain. Politics is a power game using real forces. And in this particular case the real forces you have at hand are such that you will undoubtedly be defeated. And to derive pleasure from one's own defeat is a martyromania befitting an old maid perhaps, but not politics. As a politician I have been in situations when I have had to eat humble pie and even fire itself.

It is a hellish affair to have to deal with politics, believe me, but, as you see, I have never permitted politics to be guided by my own moods, my dear comrade."

"And how far have you gone? A one-time popular leader is a lackey to a bandit and criminal type. If this testifies to your political skills, then I am grateful for your good advice. Incidentally, to make the situation easier for you, would you allow me to declare that your repertoire is known to me? In advance I can recite everything you can tell me: that people are human beings, that life is a struggle for existence, that all things should be taken as they really are, that human folly is a superpower, that the level of the proletariat depends on the level of the bourgeois class, that nature does not make leaps, and that one should reconcile oneself to the reality that walls are harder than our heads and that all cows are black at night, and why should you go off on a wild-goose chase when in life everything depends on the means of production, and the main thing is to work for the masses and not for individuals; and as for me, I am, of course, an individualist and see nothing except my own personality, my limited, petit-bourgeois modest life, and it is all a kind of art-for-art's sake, drawing-room pastime for jaded idlers, as it is impossible to advance anything through individual moralizing, and so on and so forth. And all of this is just the grinding of garbage and milling of nonsense. At the moment I am absolutely uninterested in politics. Do you understand what I have been telling you? Absolutely nothing interests me in and about politics, but if somebody already is a politician, a socialist, a royalist, and a republican, as you are, then such a man cannot teach me politics."

"And why not, may I ask?"

"Because I rank among gentlemen and not among pseudopoliticians. That's why."

Mark Antony observed me with great interest. He was not unintelligent, as a matter of fact, and for a moment it seemed to me as if in his look there was a tiny, quite insignificant dose of sympathy. Silence followed. I had a presentiment that he would rise to his feet and leave. But the man managed to pull himself together. The Minister reached mechanically for his cigarette case.

"May I?"

"Of course."

I wanted to light his cigarette, but I had no matches handy. The Minister had no match, either. I rose and opened the door to the dining room next door to bring the matches, and behind the door, taken by surprise by my quick and unexpected movement, stood the highly esteemed Agnes, my beloved wife. Concealed behind the doorway, she was eavesdropping on our conversation.

"Excuse me. I beg your pardon. We do not have a match. Please tell them to bring us the matches . . . and some brandy."

I shut the door and went back to the Minister.

The episode with my wife was most unpleasant, but it was impossible to make her invisible or to deny that she had been present. Shrugging my shoulders, I walked up and down the room two or three times and returned to the armchair without a word. The chambermaid silently made her appearance at the other door, carrying the brandy and the matches, placed both on a silver tray on the table, and, casting me a discreet and fearful glance or, rather, a horrified one, silently disappeared. I did not pay any attention to this, but it dawned on me that I had previously noticed the servants in the house watching me with horror and compassion: they believed I was mad.

In such a situation, to whom should one turn? One of our seven thousand doctors of medicine, law, or worship? One of half a million civil servants or government employees? The two hundred and fifty ministers, one of whom was now present and to top it all a

self-styled Marxist? The bronze memorials in our city? The railway-
men? The printing-plant workers? Similar popular ministers as this
one? The chambermaids? My own chambermaid called Micika, who
considered me a madman? The prostitutes?

"So, your health, Minister."

"Your health, Colleague."

We touched our glasses and emptied them and lit cigarettes; I
poured more brandy, first for the Minister and then for myself, and
once again we plunged into silence. Neither of us could find an appropriate word.

"I beg your pardon, Minister, my question may be indiscreet, but
I would like to know the following: are you going to act as Domaćinski's lawyer in this case?"

Mark Antony Javoršek was suddenly confused. A dark, almost
violet blush on his face and even on his throat appeared spontaneously. He seemed practically human. Whenever somebody suspects
that his neighbor can suffer a stroke, the candidate for death is
somehow dear to him.

"By no means. As far as I know, the indictment would bear the
signature of Mr. Hugo."

"Dr. Hugo-Hugo? He is a good lawyer. He has the reputation of
being a brilliant orator."

"Yes, he is. A dangerous opponent. And who is going to be your
lawyer?"

"I am going to be my own lawyer. In fact, I am not going to defend myself at all. I shall be satisfied with the verdict and shall not
appeal. I shall serve my prison sentence. I reckon on six or eight
months or less."

The look cast me by Minister Javoršek was the same one, partly
insecure and partly distrustful, given me by the chambermaid Micika. The man had been breathlessly watching me, and his look

betrayed more or less the following logic: What is the matter with you? Is the rumor true about your having gone mad? Does a fit of madness break out just like that, without any previous symptoms, within twenty-four hours?

Once again, silence. I poured two more brandies and silently toasted the Minister; once again we emptied our glasses and returned them to the silver tray. I poured more brandy from the bottle: first for him and then for myself.

"Thank you, Doctor, I can't take any more," the Minister said, politely touching the bottleneck with his index finger and thus symbolically rejecting my last gesture of selfless hospitality according to Chinese etiquette. Then he rose to his feet, fixing a deep, penetrating, warm, and almost direct look into my pupils, and approached me very closely. I felt the touch of his suit's woolen material and found myself inundated by his warm breath smelling of brandy and cigarettes. We stood like that, face to face, for a few seconds and then, once again, he warmly, almost intimately, bent toward me and took me by my both arms, as if I were a child. His hands were swollen and rather wet. As if caressing me, he touched my forearms from the wrists to both elbows and moved on as far as the collarbones and my nearly-double chin, then squeezed my shoulders in a friendly manner, and tapped me as if prompted by tender sympathy.

"My dear Comrade, I can't really understand you. Let us discuss the matter like close friends. In confidence, on a man-to-man basis."

"Do you want me to be absolutely frank?"

"Yes, of course, that goes without saying."

"And you won't mind if I really tell you what I have on my mind?"

"Of course not, Colleague; that, at least, is beyond discussion.

Only on the basis of absolutely sincere mutual confidence can one seriously build human relations."

"Then please sit down."

Once again we plunged into the armchairs. I lit a cigarette, realizing how he scrutinized my every gesture, even the minutest, vigilantly keeping an eye on me so that I might not hit him on the head with the bottle of brandy.

"Doctor, you've been smoking too much."

"No, this is only my third cigarette this morning. So allow me to give vent to my feelings, and my sincerity will not hurt you. All right? But I can't talk to you on a man-to-man basis because I do not trust you as a man."

The Minister, to my greatest surprise, remained perfectly calm. The tiny glittering spark in his look was gone, and the man observed me dispassionately and unpleasantly, from an unutterably great distance, the distance employed in mental clinics while inspecting the patients. At that particular moment he dominated me in every respect; his look betrayed superb intelligence and the peace of mind required at such clinics. It was the look of an old exhausted jay that had accomplished its shrieking mission a long time ago.

"Do you remember the conversation we had in the vicinity of the Evangelical Church?"

"Near the Evangelical Church, a conversation? I beg your pardon, I've forgotten about it. I've no idea what we were talking about. Really, I'm sorry, but I can't remember anything."

"I was absolutely sure you wouldn't. It was seven or eight years ago. Trifling details, logically, are quickly forgotten, a natural thing. For me that conversation between us was an unforgettable encounter, and I shall take the liberty, with your permission, to refresh your memory. Of course, on one condition."

"Yes, of course, but what is this new condition?"

"On condition that you stop scrutinizing me like a doctor or a good Samaritan, as if talking to a patient. Please, you should realize that I am not a patient and that, as I see it, there is absolutely nothing pathological in this matter. That I have gone mad can be assumed by my wife or chambermaid. But, since you've done me the honor to pay me a visit on behalf of Director-General Domaćinski, and since you already have an accusation against me and a verdict in your briefcase, as we have established, according to Paragraphs two ninety-seven, two ninety-nine, three hundred, and three o-one of the Penal Code, it would have been logical for you to reject the allegation about my mental incompetence. For what would have been the purpose of an accusation based on Paragraph three o-one of the Penal Code if it were aimed at someone irresponsible, someone believed to be an insane slanderer?

"Let us move on to our conversation near the Evangelical Church. It was an unusually hot day, one of those nasty days in our subalpine warm weather when asphalt melts under the soles of our shoes, when sweat sticks to the feet and the shoulder blades, when the female smell is intensely sensed in the streets, so that the whole town smells like a girls' high school. The wind blows, raising clouds of dust. The leaves on the branches had extracted the last drop of moisture from their stems so that you heard them rubbing against each other and cracking as if sclerosis had broken out among them, and a whole alley of chestnuts had sunk, as if bewitched, covered with ashes, buried under lava, filthy, dusty, sticky. It was all illuminated by a red overhead quartz lamp and there were pastel-blue shades, unearthly, like a genuine hellish fire, and everything was nothing less than our own pure, real, not-at-all artificial inferno of so-called summer heat we long for so eagerly. On such a day we met in the shade of a row of trees right in front of the Evangelical

Church. Please forgive me if I mention one other detail, which is of vital significance to me. It was my impression of you on that day, and it is of fundamental importance in my personal distrust of you: you emerged from the shadow of that row of trees wearing a raw silk suit, white shoes, striped tie, a Panama hat, a silk shirt; you were fresh from the bath, shaved, sprayed with eau de cologne, still relatively young, slim, full of vitality, smiling pleasantly after the first morning cigarette, and, it seemed to me, healthy and carefree. In brief, a genuine Socialist minister, a careerist who has his dividends, his solid and profitable job with, naturally, a capitalist cartel, his social relations, his career that would last a long time, and who moves about the world cheerfully, even triumphantly, indeed victoriously. In our vicinity, in a trench three and a half meters deep, in a seventy-five-centimeter-wide cave, workers were laying gas pipelines. The whole row of trees around the Evangelical Church floated in a cloud of filthy, smoky gas, and down below, at the bottom of that muddy grave, the stinking smell must have been unbearable, since those half-naked ragamuffins climbed to the surface every other minute to take a breath of fresh air, removing from their noses some muddy rags, some sort of handkerchiefs they had tied over them to protect themselves against the revolting smell of the gas, which was so bad that by comparison bad eggs smelled like amber. In every other civilization those innocent people, who are actually sentenced to imprisonment at hard labor, or rather lifelong imprisonment at forced labor, would have been given some sort of protective masks, but in our country they were pushed to work in that noisome place with filthy rags stuck in their mouths. What had impressed me even more than these shipwrecks were their overcoats hanging from the fence of the Evangelical Church. These clothes, worn in the Zagorje and Medjumurje regions, were old and worn out, and bread and onions could be seen sticking out of the pockets.

Noon time in a very hot summer. Around us those resurrected Lazaruses inhaled the sticky, dusty, suffocating, and smelly heat like a drop of a precious elixir, masked burglars who had dragged themselves exhausted into the sun like dying cats gathering around a fire.

"We shook hands and I drew your attention to the rags on the fence of the church and to the loaves of bread sadly sticking out of the torn, lifeless sleeves; in another civilization the supervisors concerned would have provided gas masks, but here, look what the wardrobe of our proletariat is like. If nothing else, then those filthy rags on the fence provided evidence of the mess in which we live. 'And you are still sentimental, Doctor' was more or less what you said in reply to me. 'That's romanticism from the 'eighties of the last century. By lamenting over their fate we are not going to help them. I am not at all sorry for them. They feel better than we do.' 'How do you mean? I don't understand you. Who feels better than we?' I asked. 'They feel better than we intellectuals, we white-collar proletariat,'—that was your answer. . . . 'These miserable creatures earning eighteen dinars a day get eighty per cent more than they need. Nine dinars is sufficient for meeting all their needs. And we, Colleague, do not earn even thirty per cent of the cost of the standard of living pertaining to intellectuals of our rank in Europe. Why should I be sorry for this filthy illiterate Balkan flesh? I'm sorry for myself, Doctor, I'm sorry for you, and not for those wretched people. They are happy, they have no needs, they snore beautifully throughout the winter in a warm house where they cook their stinking sausages. Don't lament, please. It's Hamlet-like behavior.' . . . I don't guarantee that I've quoted your words accurately, but this is more or less what you said. I knew you as a Socialist, as a Socialist Minister, as a popular leader, as an orator at mass meetings, and as, so to speak, a Marxist, and I simply remarked, without any ulterior motive, that your outlook on the given situation was not a hundred-per-cent Marxist."

" 'All right, what do you mean? Do I swear by Marx? Marx wrote his analysis eighty years ago and I have been troubling you with my own promissory notes today. I have never been a Marxist monist, Doctor. On principle, I don't believe in any dogma.'

" 'As for myself, I've never been a Marxist, Minister. Good-by.'

"This was how we parted seven years ago and from that time until now, as far as I can remember, we've never had an opportunity, apart from the most banal and conventional phrases, to exchange any real, human ideas, and now, suddenly, you insist that I should completely trust you as a man. I don't trust you, I can't trust you; I would be lying if I told you that I trusted you, and, in my view, to admit that is the most logical thing to do. . . ."

Minister Javoršek took a long time to extinguish his cigarette in the ashtray and, when he raised his head and did me the honor to look at me once again, he seemed to have grown tired and rather bored: exhausted, blasé, an old veteran who had often participated in unpleasant affairs of this kind.

"In spite of the convincingly sentimental undertone of your account of our conversation near the Evangelical Church, I can only vaguely remember the encounter when, in a raw silk suit, I appeared to you young and fresh, and in a triumphant mood. If that occurred seven years ago, as you put it, then, unfortunately, facts prove just the contrary: I was deep in debt, in the middle of a very intricate crisis, about to divorce my second wife; my left kidney had been taken out around Easter. In brief, it was all a mistaken assumption on your part. I don't deny a single one of the words you've just quoted like a gramophone record. I could very well have spoken like that, since what I said then corresponds with my present views. I am not an immature man and I am not burning with the first

fervent support of Marxism as you are, my dear landlord. You
should rather allow me to tell you on a normal man-to-man basis
that this sort of talk is nothing but a kind of masturbation. It is
talking like a parrot, pointlessly. It's silly to denounce someone as
a criminal type for having shot a burglar in self-defense, especially
at a time when anarchy prevailed on all sides like a plague. Not to
trust somebody only because one morning he happened to walk in
the shade of a row of trees in a raw silk suit? What sense is there
in that? Don't talk like that, please. It makes me think of a hysterical old maid with an unsettled sex life. It's not the way a citizen
should think, an individual who should care about his own dignity
as a man."

"I beg your pardon, did you come to my house to collect a piece
of information or to insult me? I've accepted my notice and, as for
the accusation, it has been brought to my knowledge. To say anything else is unnecessary, Minister. You may leave the house by
walking through the middle door. Good-by."

I rose and slammed the door to the dining room.

Leaning against the cupboard, in tears, with a handkerchief crum-
pled between her fingers, stood Agnes. Everything suggested a great
scene, but it all ended unexpectedly quickly, like a tooth extraction
under Novocain—by the time you open your eyes, the tooth is out.
She began in a melodramatic way: I had ruined our happiness,
along with our children's future; in brief, everything that had been
the whole purpose of her existence. She could not carry on like this
any longer. She did not want to. Out, out!

Between the dinner in the vineyard and this ultimate "Out, out!"
five days had elapsed. The dinner party had been on Saturday; and
on Tuesday I sent a letter to Domaćinski; on Wednesday Mark Antony Javoršek made the appointment for our historical meeting and

then, the next day, Thursday, came the break with Agnes. From
Sunday to Thursday, judging by its external manifestations, life in
our house was completely normal. Everybody was perhaps slightly
more polite than before, and practically deaf and dumb, but the
performance was carried on as it always was. To the clinking of cut-
lery against the chinaware on the table and facing bowed heads and
nervous looks ("Look, strange things have been going on with
Father, he's showing signs of abnormality"), I behaved with Agnes
and the girls as if nothing had happened. I pretended not to notice
their suspicions that something, if I may put it so, had disturbed my
spiritual equilibrium. So, at our wits' end, we played a very complicated and dangerous game. I pretended not to know the children
knew something that they could not know, and the children, in their
turn, pretended not to know what was notorious, what all the servants in the kitchen were talking about, and what their mother had
also confirmed to them: that something had been going on with
their father, and that he should be put in an asylum. In the meantime I had never been alone with Agnes (for two or three years
now we had been sleeping in separate rooms), and at that moment,
in the dining room, when she was not wearing the mask, in spite of
my dignity I betrayed my petit-bourgeois narrow-mindedness; I admit, I was not master of the situation. Overwhelmed by the realization that she had been eavesdropping and irritated to some extent
by the conversation with Javoršek, I was sharper and more logical
with her than I should have been. In fact, we had come to the liqui-
dation of a marriage that was just about ready for its silver wedding anniversary.

"Well, may I repeat it, please, just to summarize what you have
been saying: All of you around me agree that for more than a year
now I have been provoking everybody, taking advantage of every
given situation, maintaining that Domaćinski had shot four men,

that he had been boasting of it for the seven hundred and seventy-seventh time, that he had voiced his regret at not having shot me too like a mad dog, that he had attacked me with a revolver in hand, and that he would indeed probably have shot me like a dog had I not run away like a dog. In this you are all in agreement with Domaćinski, with his goggled-eyed cow of a wife, his scoundrel lawyer, with all those idiots around us, with all those monkeys and druggists, that is, that I should be put in an asylum only because I once dared speak my mind. And now you are threatening me with an ultimatum: either surrender and ask pardon from all of you, or take the consequences. In your view, it is not in my interest or in the interests of my children that you be under the protection of an idiot, of a high-strung and overwrought neurotic man. You think that that baritone of yours would bring up my children better than I—who do not know how to be grateful to my benefactors? You see, Domaćinski treated me well, and I spat in his face. I am provoking public scandals in the parks, the mob was rushing behind the cab taking me to the police. I put out my tongue at old Floriani. I told Minister Harambašević to his face that he stole stamps. I have ruined my existence. My marriage. My children's happiness. And now, amid all this intricate confusion—out I go. Must I either admit that I went mad—not completely, but nevertheless, twenty-five percent—and with seventy-five percent of my common sense regret the whole case, put right all those outbreaks, remedy the situation at least to some extent with my repentance, or realize that I have no right to threaten the peace and happiness of my family any further? I see. I am going to leave. I consent to a divorce. I shall bear the blame for it. And I am especially pleased not to be obliged to sit any longer at the opera listening to "Carmen" and expressing my admiration for Escamillo. Don't be afraid. I am not a Don José. Good-by."

5

SCANDAL
IN THE HOTEL

At the Hotel Europe I became the occupant of Room 242, but this,
I must say, was not particularly amusing. In those days none of the
books I had been dragging about with me for many years could
mean anything to me. Neither Erasmus nor Buddha, nor even St.
Augustine can completely take Platonic blame for the adultery of
a moment's caprice; and at that time I was looking for a special
book that might teach me what to do next in the complex situation
in which I found myself.

In the provincial crucible of our so-called liberalism, my unexpected moving to a hotel, making no secret of having parted from

my wife Agnes due to my own fault, had heightened the general dissatisfaction with my personality, which is unworthy of such exaggerated attention. And when, in conversation with an old acquaintance of mine, Dr. Werner, a prominent editor-in-chief, freethinker, and Mason, who had attacked me frontally, saying that I "should have been put in an asylum for my own benefit because I was doing such obviously stupid things contrary to my own interests," I replied that he was a tasteless Philistine, he began to mutter something about Europe, about the European way of thought, about the European duties of citizens toward themselves. However, when I questioned him, he could not give one single reason why my conduct had been that of an abnormal, pathological fool and not in keeping with European standards.

Hell! What in my behavior was not European? Was I not an inhabitant of Europe? Wasn't I, on top of that, living in a hotel named after Europe? Furthermore, what have I done? I told a bandit that he was a bandit and that was about all. Why did I say this to the crook? Because he declared his intention of shooting me like a dog. Why didn't I tell him that even earlier? I don't know. Also, why, apart from me, had nobody else told him? What I had said was only the opinion of the whole town—it did not have to be demonstrated to Werner, whose opinion also was in no way different from mine. The only thing was that nobody wanted to say it in public. Why? For a thousand reasons. Had I not spoken my mind, nothing would have been changed. Because I spoke my mind, I was dismissed from my job and was going to be put on trial; I had shouldered the guilt for an adultery I had not committed; I lived in a hotel because, after all, I had to live somewhere. "And now, my dear friend, as a freethinker and a Mason, as a representative of the liberal, broad-minded press, you have been talking to me about 'Europe' in an overheated and arbitrary fashion. What 'Europe?' I would like just once to hear what that Europe is in reality. Where is that Europe situated? What does that Europe want? And in what special relationship with that Europe are you? Have you gained any special privileges so that you, personally, all on your own, can refer to Europe? It is as if you, personally, are both its legal and moral representative, whereas I am not. How have I offended that Europe? When? Why?"

"My dear Doctor, calm down, please. I did not mean to hurt you. No doubt you are absolutely right. Yes, without doubt. But, considering the circumstances, and so on and so forth . . ."

"I know. Yes, certainly. . . . I know it all. But can we please first establish the facts: I am seated at my table in the café where I have been sitting for the second week. I was reading a newspaper when you were so kind as to honor me, on your own initiative, with your presence; you interrupted my reading and we faced each other like two absolutely equal tavern guests, with the sole difference that you joined me at my table and not I you at yours. You have just one single right: to rise to your feet, to say good-by, and to go. This is the right that belongs to you, and this is the only thing you are not denied by me. However, as far as my jurisdiction is concerned, I most energetically dissociate myself from any right of yours to teach me or to calm me, especially when you have no reason for it. To my mind no statement of yours like 'but, and so on . . .' is a valid argument. I am not irritated, I am not upset at all; I am completely calm; I beg you to believe that all assumptions about the ruined state of my nerves are completely unfounded. I did not land in this situation on account of my nerves, but because of logic. And as you have begun poking your nose into my married life, please remember that I broke off my relations with my wife as a cuckold who had been laughed at as such by the town for a whole year. Shall I now accuse the mother or the so-called mother of my children of adul-

tery in court after that same lady has persuaded even my own children that I am mad?

"By the way, I don't know whether you still remember: at the
close of 1918, when you were the editor of *The Scales,* a weekly
dealing with cultural and political matters, and I was still in uni-
form as an Austrian army officer, I brought you an article entitled
'Give Us a Thousand Men,' and you rejected that first attempt of
mine because 'it was brilliantly written, and could be a first-rate
contribution to the paper but, and so forth. . . .' You see, that phrase
of yours—'but, and so forth'—has been between us for eighteen
years and in that respect nothing has changed in our mutual relations. It so happened that I passed over that Philistine 'but, and so
forth,' and yet you threaten me with an asylum in the interests of a
'Europe' that you yourself know nothing about—neither its morals,
interests, God, family, ideological pattern, 'and so forth, but. . . .'"

Dr. Werner smiled kindly, and this should have meant he had
stripped off his mask and at least for a moment revealed his real
face. Amazingly, he still remembered my article "Give Us a Thousand Men," and that recollection from the year 1918 had visibly
warmed him. A man of exceptional memory, he paraphrased more
than two-thirds of my work. Apparently, Dr. Werner was particularly pleased to talk about the days when he seemed to himself an
imposing, magnificent lighthouse in the darkness of history.

Toward the end of the first World War, Dr. Werner began to
spread the network of his ideas, outlooks, proposals, and programs.
From his reeking printshop every Friday his paper, *The Scales,*
stretched its wings over our muddy land, illusions fluttered over our
glens and revived the dearest hopes for freedom, equality, and
brotherhood. At the same time *The Scales* became increasingly pros-
perous; subscriptions arrived in growing number, its influence on
so-called public opinion spread and was more and more visible: the

lectures, the talks, the babbling about cooperatives, the cooperative movement, the founding of consumer unions, labor unions, the movements, the parties, the masses, the universal suffrage, the elections, the mandates, the success of the mandate that exceeds everything in importance. . . .

One day a young artillery officer made his appearance in the editorial offices of *The Scales,* having arrived via Budapest directly from the Ukrainian border, bearded, wearing a filthy, wrinkled, heavy military raincoat, jangling his spurs, and carrying a big cavalry saber. He had brought Dr. Werner a project based on the wartime experience of an intellectual titled "Give Us a Thousand Men."

Amid that mire of ours through which greasy waters flowed as thick as blood soup and where everything was suffocated in its own dirt, all our ideas were adjusted to the petit-bourgeois realities in which everybody was full of roast suckling pig, barbecued pork, venison cooked to suit the hunter's taste with cream and berries, woodcock, pheasant, partridge, lamb, turkey, Riesling, Reutsch Mineral Water, brandy, and a special outlook on life. And amid the excessive drinking, entertaining, gossiping and repeating of other people's business secrets, a young artillery officer sought a thousand souls from Dr. Werner and *The Scales* because, unless that thousand found its way to the masses, unless it discovered ways of digging the foundations of a new universal humanistic structure here, on our own land, everything would remain unchanged, as it was in the past, with the sole difference that, instead of the Counts Khuen or Tisza or Franz Josef I, some new faces would rule, whereas the situation under the Huns would continue to exist within the context of a revived Tartaric, Hungarian state. Surrounded by a confused, uneducated, petty, short-sighted, narrow-minded, cunning quasi-intelligentsia, we should have at least a thousand people who were worried about the moral trap they were in—who saw that one day they themselves might be trapped by their own contradictions or by some social success that would eventually amount to a negation of everything that now seemed to them the ideal. For we idealists cannot have it as an ideal to become rich scoundrels who grow fat eating the bait from their own traps in high posts. This kind of national liberation would be no liberation. The only way out is to develop a free contemporary individual, and so forth, of course, but. . . .

"Yes, you see, but that 'and so forth, of course, but . . .' was exactly what did not suit you. I don't say it might have been more intelligent of you to have been wasting your time on the battlefields, but if people are at war, then it is far better to fight shoulder to shoulder with them, regardless of how maddening it may be, than to lose your nerve in lonely rooms, especially if you're a leader, a public worker, a politician, the initiator, the editor-in-chief. I remember that in 1918—in early spring—I know that, because sometime in early March I was transferred from the Ukrainian sector to the staff replacement depot in Ljubljana—there was a feeling that we had no stronghold, foundation, or basis: we were in fear of the brutal military force of the Central Powers, in terror of guerrilla anarchy, and panic-stricken in the face of our domestic vacuum. That stupid imperialistic war revealed to us how we had been living in cycles of historical defeats and how all those catastrophes had not, unfortunately, taken place without evil results. You quoted Herzen—I remember, it was really Herzen you referred to—and the fact that I had been seeking the first thousand souls who would be the first phalanx, followed by hundreds more, seemed to you sheer imagination, an adventure, totally unrealistic and romantic, too much of a challenge, a risk. And today? The romantic wartime illusions from the years 1917–18 are far behind us, in the distant and already historical past, and what has come out of it all? You have had two legitimate wives, three mistresses, thirty-three unpleasant affairs; you bought your wives necklaces, gold bracelets, expensive carpets; you supported eleven different governments; you have your own limousine, your villa, your debts, loans, funds, new credits; you are the editor of the most outstanding paper, now financed by Domaćinski, who is a symbol, and you are disturbed because some kind of paranoiac dared declare to that financier of yours that he was a bandit. It is all semiconsciousness and drunkenness and debauchery.

"And may I ask just one thing of you: Stop, my dear friend, playing the annoying role of a preacher. May honor be done to you and to all the funds at your own disposal. For a whole lifetime you have been buying souls at two or three cents apiece but, nevertheless, and so forth, what is the purpose of all this talk? Two worlds, two criteria, two logics, two mentalities. To avoid all misunderstanding: I have never been a moralist and on no condition do I intend to become one. Just the opposite—I have my own bizarre notion of the world of moral values: to my mind, the question of morals is a matter of taste. The only measure of wisdom, it seems to me today, is the measure of form. Today, as far as the individual is concerned, there is nothing in the world that has not been disfigured. A lack of taste amounts to a lack of wisdom. In reality, everything that is full of vitality, that is, determined by nature, cannot be anything but harmonious and tasteful. In our country, just take a cross section of the life of anyone of our people, I don't care if they are average or prominent. Everything is tasteless. When this Domaćinski of yours began howling at me to shut up, it appeared tasteless to me to fall silent in front of that troglodyte who knew of no other imperative but that of a revolver. And when it came to a situation in which my wife, after twenty-four years of married life, asked me to repent, although I knew with the clearest conscience that I had done nothing wrong so that I had nothing to repent of, I told her to go to hell. I do not care what people around us think. You have to know what our neighbors consider as lyricism, what paintings they paint, how they live in their houses and apartments, what politics they pursue, to realize that it is all mostly a universal lack of good taste. People in our country worry about their digestions, hemorrhoids, folklore, careers, politics, with nothing in their heads and water in their veins. I have never been surprised, therefore, if the average butcher or patriot in our country thought there was no other musical instrument than a *tamburitza,* but I did not expect to come across a Werner among all these bewildered moralists. If a moralist is bewildered, you ought to be able to expect him to know how to express his viewpoint in terms different from those that I can hear every day from my fellow citizens: paranoia, nerves, dignity, reputation, and the like: perfectly pointless—how shall I put it?—prejudices."

To my greatest surprise, Dr. Werner did not apologize for having trusted the rumors about my mental equilibrium. Instead, the old man became sentimental and said he was really most pleased to have found out my condition for himself. He fully realized the deep, practically symbolic logic of my behavior. He did not share my opinion in everything, but he was liberal enough to understand my case.

He realized he was not talking to an overstrained neurasthenic, for he suddenly put a completely sober, civil question to me: he had heard that I was selling my three-storied house, and he wanted to know whether it was true. He was personally interested in the matter and would immediately explain why.

"Yes, I am selling the three-story house at Bishop Square for one million and three hundred thousand."

He knew the house, and the price was in the main agreeable to him, he would send his lawyer to see me tomorrow. . . .

"Dr. Hugo-Hugo?"

"Yes, Hugo-Hugo."

"Please do not. I don't want to see that gentleman."

"May one know why?"

"Domaćinski's lawyer. . . ."

He was not altogether pleased by this link to Domaćinski because he himself had business connections with Dr. Hugo-Hugo. But, excuse him. He asked me twice to excuse him because he did not have the slightest bad feeling toward me—he felt for me nothing but the purest sympathy, which he had nurtured for me uninterruptedly over the years. He had been prompted exclusively by my interests, though on a mistaken assumption, and he would be only too pleased if we managed to settle, to our mutual satisfaction, our possible common business in the form of a contract on sale and purchase, and so forth—"Good-by."

"Good-by, dear Doctor."

During the whole conversation, "Yes, of course, but, and so forth," next to my table, immediately behind me, was sitting Mrs. Jadviga Jesenska.

She was a woman of about forty-seven, a fat brunette weighing well over a hundred and seventy-five pounds, in the late autumn of a rich but faded beauty, a woman whose lawyer I had been six or seven years earlier in a very intricate inheritance case. A shipwrecked woman, Jadviga Jesenska lived in the same Hotel Europe on the same floor as I, in Room 246, and it was rumored in the city that she had been living there as a kind of hotel employee, a so-called lady to keep company with the more distinguished foreign guests who seek not only a love affair but want a well-brought-up, witty, and cultured person to talk to. Jadviga Jesenska had three or four marriages behind her, several suicides in which, it was rumored, she had played a fatal role, and she herself had attempted suicide after an unpleasant affair involving cocaine trafficking, but in court her innocence was confirmed; she had traveled abroad, kept gambling houses in better hotels, and this evening she was bored. Leaning back in her chair so close to me that I could feel the warmth of her cheeks, she asked me as usual whether I felt like playing a game of chess.

Since I had moved to the Hotel Europe, I had played at least thirty games of chess with Jadviga Jesenska. I lost regularly: either she extricated her queen or it seemed that she would do so. She was certainly more composed and cleverer; from the very first move she dominated the chessboard, pretending skillfully in a very sly way that she was playing with an equal.

I did not feel like playing. That evening, at least so it appeared to me, I was too absent-minded to play chess. It was a rainy, tedious evening and Jadviga Jesenska felt the need for something. So we moved on to the Club Bar. After either the seventh or eighth glass of whiskey, she admitted having listened to the conversation between me and Dr. Werner. Until now she had been perfectly discreet with me, never mentioning my case. But at the Club Bar, while drinking whiskey, she confessed that she fully agreed to everything I had said to her first husband, the old reprobate Dr. Werner, especially everything about morals and taste. She was closely acquainted with that highly cultured school of bourgeois moralists. She had to deal with them in gambling houses and in bed: they were the most flagrant swine, those so-called moralists.

While sipping the eleventh glass of whiskey, I sensed the softness, warmth, and tenderness of her fingers; her elbows as cool as camphor, the silky curls, pleasant-smelling hair, the charm, all plump and rounded, though a little too big, with massive, swollen calves—solid, dear, witty. Everything ended in her room, number

246, exactly according to customary hotel rules: the obligatory
squeaking of the bed, then the noise of the waterpipes from the
bathroom while I was half asleep, and the dull return to Room 242,
carrying various objects: my umbrella, spats, overcoat, trousers—I
did not know where my hat was, or my watch and chain: whether
I had forgotten my wallet, what had happened to my left garter,
or where the newspaper was. The cigarettes were there, and the
matches and the necktie, but where was the key? Of course there
was no light, the elevator was buzzing, someone was coming from
the other end of the corridor. How ridiculous. Hotel corridors exist
in the world to enable hotel guests to pass through them. . . .

My trifling adventure with Jadviga Jesenska developed into a
whole series of the most shocking scandals. That the two of us
should play chess in one of the most prominent cafés in town
had disturbed our moralists to such an extent that the café, which
was usually empty between ten and twelve at night, began to be
crowded with guests: the aristocracy, the university professors—
deans, assistant professors, Ph.D's—their wives, the Senator from
Hyperion Balenteković Street, and the unavoidable Dr. Hugo-Hugo.
Everybody arrived in the Café Europe between nine and twelve at
night for a small cup of coffee with cream. One night, about midnight, after her grandson Egon von Sarvaš went to the café as an
advance guard, even the old wife of General Aquacurti-Sarvaš-
Daljski made her appearance there, although up to that time she
had displayed no particular interest in the development of the
queen's gambit. To play chess under the eyes of that curious,
malicious, spying pack was not fun, and that was why we moved
on to the Club Bar. As chess is not played over there, we drank
whiskey and saw to our dismay professors, rectors, deans, assistants,
and their wives appear in the Club Bar and, like the tetanus

bacillus that is constantly present, so was Dr. Hugo-Hugo. It was so crowded that a tubercular xylophone player asked the bar manager for a pay raise, assuming mistakenly that the increased attendance in the night club was the result of her playing. We then took refuge in a remote bar on the outskirts of the town but were discovered there, too. We had to change five more bars and, at last, we returned to the Europe, but in vain; they followed us everywhere. Thereupon Mrs. Jadviga Jesenska and I decided to drive every Sunday in an open car to a silent mass in one of the more distinguished churches in the upper section of the town, and this aroused universal dissatisfaction that led to a whole torrent of anonymous letters.

Jadviga Jesenska, an old, experienced, tested expert in receiving anonymous correspondence, assured me that the letters were from my wife Agnes and her friends. My wife was not satisfied with my taking, like a real gentleman, the whole blame for a non-existent guilt. She was compelled by a deep moral need to express constant horror over my immoral, unhealthy, mad way of life that she herself had very wisely abandoned in time, like a sinking ship. I took for granted what Jadviga Jesenska had suggested, i.e., that, unfortunately, the anonymous letters could really have been from my wife or her friends. I believed Jadviga Jesenska in everything that concerned women and their mysterious conduct. Jadviga Jesenska was extremely well acquainted with women's nature, she being a rare case and having a characteristic unusual in women: Jadviga Jesenska was profoundly ashamed of being a woman. The main secret of her success and charm perhaps stemmed from this bizarre feeling of worthlessness. She gave herself to her friends, stretching herself out like a carpet, did it with a silent and unfeigned sense of guilt that even if it was only a trick, was nevertheless an effective one. Jadviga Jesenska did not rank among the women who can easily be forgotten. As a little girl, in the loneliness of her maiden's

bed, she was ashamed of her small lovers from the dancing school
who dragged themselves below her window shivering with cold
under the gas lights like curly-haired dogs. She despised women
from her early childhood and even rebuffed her own mother, so that
she spent her life in complete loneliness. All the elderly women in
her early childhood at her grandmother's in the provinces moved
about like monsters in chemises, with candles in hand, either fighting the fleas or in intimate relationship with a chamber pot underneath their beds. Everything about those pious old matrons in her
earliest childhood was false: the hair, the corsets, the teeth, the
morals, and the piety. In brief, they consisted only of pressed
breasts, cushioned hips, waists bound by corsets, false convictions,
lack of common sense in their heads, and plenty of malice in their
hearts. In the orchard at her grandmother's, she saw the cowgirl
called Anna pissing beneath her skirt while standing under a cherry
tree. She was so disturbed by that experience, which was actually a
normal and every-day occurrence, that from that time her image of
a woman was regularly connected with one and the same scene: the
picture of a cowgirl in a blue cotton pleated skirt, her legs spread,
standing above a warm waterfall. That dreadful woman without a
corset and without any morals, a woman without any feigned hy-
pocrisy, pissing whenever the need arose, created a repugnance toward unrefined women that has survived in Jadviga up to this day.

At the turn of the century, her girlhood coincided in time with
a still semi-feudal and quasi-guild system, as backward as life in a
harem; and so Jadviga, in all probability, was one of the first
women in our country to dare to light a cigarette in the most public
place in our town, the café. In reality, those first cigarettes smoked
in public by Jadviga Jesenska were a pioneer action at a time when
every coach was closely watched at night to find out who was in it,
when nobody was interested in knowing who individual people

were and what their profession was, but rather who their fathers were, since it was considered a token of nobility to have a father who was an intellectual or, for instance, a secretary or court clerk in the royal national government. The son of such a distinguished court clerk in the national government, Dr. Benjamin Skalinski, a law student, a young man of twenty-one, committed suicide, and blame for the death of that young man was placed on Jadviga Jesenska, who was under seventeen at the time. They discovered a whole bunch of love letters young Skalinski had written to Jadviga and, judging from the very tone, the motives, and the insanely explicit description of some pornographic details, it was beyond doubt there had been a fantastic, unhealthy, obscure, stormy, and genuinely bodily intercourse between the two. During the moral investigation carried out by Secretary Skalinski, Benjamin's mother, Madame Lucia, who had instinctively disliked Jadviga as her possible future daughter-in-law from the very first day, made compromising statements about Jadviga: that she had often come to their house, that she had often gone out for long walks with the young man who had committed suicide, and that, on one occasion, when she entered her son's room unexpectedly, she found the girl sitting on the boy's knees. Jadviga tried to deny these insinuations and persistently stuck to her first deposition: that she had no idea of it at all, that she had never received any of the compromising letters, that nothing mentioned in the letters did or could have occurred; in brief, Jadviga denied everything.

She had been in contact with Skalinski through her mother, who was a bosom friend of Mrs. Skalinski. The late Benjamin had, by the way, told her they would announce their engagement after he passed his examinations. But she, personally, had never attached any particular importance to this because the pretentious young man had never in any way appealed to her.

The Skalinskis had an old-fashioned drawing room right out of the eighties; the curtains were made of opaque, dark red cotton drawn aside by wooden rings on a rod, so that whenever anybody pulled the curtains, the rings clattered in a muffled way like small skeletons. Because of those unpleasant curtains and the uncomfortably dark corridor, which was regularly inundated by the smell of spices and the lavatory, and because of the dark, polished door that only intensified the dark, unpleasant atmosphere, and especially because of the spoiled raspberry juice that smelled like washed baby diapers, and because of Benjamin, who would whisper indecent words to her, she had never liked that apartment, those visits, Mrs. Skalinski, or anybody in that unpleasant family. Once, when she had brought some cakes as a gift to Mrs. Skalinski (her mother often used to send her with warm cakes wrapped in a napkin and a message from the first to the second floor) and when they were alone for a minute in the red drawing room, Benjamin tried, with a decisive gesture, to pinch her left thigh under her skirt above the garter, but she threatened to rouse everybody in the house and he withdrew his hand. He once leaped like an animal to the window, grabbed the canary cage, and threw it into the garden. . . .

The moralists at the police station listened to the statement by the little girl and nobody believed a single word she said. A policeman with gold-rimmed spectacles ordered her to go to the room next door and take off all her clothes. After an examination, they established that she was a virgin and let her go home, crushed, violated, and despised. That was how her life began, a life now coming to an end in the better hotels. To make the mess even worse, her mother, an old-fashioned confused hen (the widow of a provincial surveyor, who was her elder by twenty-seven years), attempted to throw herself under a train, but fainted near the railroad and was found at night lying in the mud by passers-by. After that incident, her mother lived only for another six months, and after the funeral Jadviga, being barred from all the secondary schools, was completely alone in the small town with the poplars, with green lights on foggy railroad tracks, and tiring walks along the fences on the outskirts of town where barking dogs could be heard and gas lamps squinted at lonely passers-by. Everything was plunged into obscurity around her, submerged by the dark footprints of her broken-hearted walking, and she did not know what she should really do. From that day till now, this small town seemed to her an unutterably painful walk along strangers' fences; that lonely, aimless walk in the small town was regularly repeated—three hundred sixty times from one fall to the next—and the futile walking evolved into an unbelievable, mysterious, one-sided picture of the sadness of a woman's life that has passed without a single event worth living.

What had really happened? Scandals, sheer scandals and disgrace. Indigestion, headaches, cramps in the womb, ailing kidneys, nerves, monetary worries, and troubles in general, a whole series of love affairs and abortions, bridge parties in smoky gambling houses. Bridge parties with rich old women jingling with diamond bracelets and judging one another by the value of a pearl necklace, flabby, with heavy makeup, clumsy, disgusting old women smelling of sweetish urine and applying strong deodorants, who did not know anything about card games and spent whole nights talking about their servants, preserves, good hotels abroad. These overdressed potbellies in costly furs buried under ribbons and makeup observed things around them in the light of that limited, odious *entre-nous* atmosphere that is revolting, sickening, and insane: *"Entre nous,* please, who bought that woman her fox stole? And her brooch? And her bracelet? And her villa? And her car?"

Now, let us find out what is more decent: to gain a bracelet, a

villa, a car, horses, servants, ships, summer resorts, jewelry, securi-
ties, and become a distinguished lady or to gain nothing?

Jadviga earned no villas. On that ground alone she was considered a loose woman. If she had lived in her own villa, she would
have been a distinguished lady. No, nobody has any strong, truthful,
heroic convictions in life. Nobody has any character. Convictions
and character are nothing but sentimental news of the day, and
that rubbish is put on sale at newsstands and read in lavatories and
is what is called moral standards.

Walking along the muddy street, Jadviga was overwhelmed by
a soft, dim sadness about growing old—a sadness creeping over her
like the monotonous autumn rain. It became increasingly and strik-
ingly clear to her that the people around her were deaf and rheumatic, breathed laboriously and found it ever more difficult to bend
to reach something they had dropped. . . . Everything was worn out
about people: they complained about debts; they were involved in
gossip; they had five-storied houses built; they traded in large objects; they bought ships, mines, vineyards; at bridge parties they
lamented worriedly and falsely about being too busy; everybody
talked about his work, whereas, in fact, nobody did anything; people played bridge and for whole nights groaned for a moment of
love.

Without any special preoccupations, Jadviga Jesenska moved
along the streets watching the windows of a green one-storied house
and the shadows of pine trees quivering on its walls washed by the
rain. The house thus seemed to her mysterious, and so it was out of
the question that an obscure and fatal affair had taken place within
it. Overwhelmed by distrust and superstition, she was annoyed by
trifles: that somebody with rubber heels had silently and sneakily
slipped past her, or that a goitrous woman had bleated like a kid

while her goiter jumped like a living thing out of her dirty collar.
A boy had appeared under her balcony on the previous night carrying a drum wrapped in black cloth and that sight made her burst
into tears. Half-lowered blinds in a window on the north side of
the street evoked an unpleasant and suspicious thought that somebody in that room was telling dangerous lies and concocting intrigues that were a danger to herself or somebody connected with
her. The whole previous afternoon she had tried to imagine the face
of that unknown person, had dreamed about nuns, about a corridor in a hospital where fish were moving about in hospital gar-
ments, and also how somebody had taken out his gold teeth with
two fingers, and a beam of light had illuminated the metal horse-
shoe-shaped teeth. And all morning she had been shuffling cards
for solitaire, and every time the jack of clubs came up, signifying
bad news in the house or an event that would in all probability be
unpleasant.

I have never believed in cards but it came out that Jadviga's jack
of clubs really did mean bad news. Several nights later, while I
was asleep in my room, Number 242, there was a knock at the door
—a rather indiscreet and impertinent knock.

"Who is it?"

"The police!"

"What police?"

"In the name of the law, the police! Open up!"

Jadviga, without anything on, completely naked, too lazy to get
up, drew the eiderdown over her head and muttered something
about tasteless swine. I got up, also completely naked, and as inno-
cently as Adam unlocked the door.

"Well, what do you want?"

"What are you doing, have you gone mad?" somebody asked me
from the poorly illuminated corridor.

"I am sleeping as a hotel guest in my own bed, involved in promiscuity, if you don't mind. And what about you, who are you, if I may ask?"

"We're from the morals squad."

"Is that so? Glad to meet you. Please come in. Do you want us to sign some sort of statement perhaps? Or jump through the window? Enroll in the Salvation Army?"

The toothless, pimply face smiled in the twilight, lifted a creased cap, and disappeared to the far end of the corridor without saying a word. The other one who had told me he was a member of the police responsible for morals stopped for another moment, gazing straight into my eyes, as if about to ask an important, almost fatal question; then he turned round with the obvious intention of leaving, but then once again returned to the threshold and peeped curiously into the room, stumbling as if at a loss as to what he was supposed to do in such a situation.

Jadviga Jesenska sat up in bed, threw away the eiderdown, and stuck out her tongue.

"And this is who you have been sleeping with?"

"Yes, this is who I have been sleeping with. And what are you going to do next?"

As I was not very shrewd, it was only now that it dawned on me that everything might have been staged: "And you, who are you? Show me your warrant."

"My colleague has the warrant."

"Oh, your colleague. And where is your colleague? Where has he disappeared to? It would have been better for him to stay here if he wanted to check on people sleeping in hotels."

"He went to fetch an officer to take you to jail."

"Is that so? Then wait a minute until I dress myself. If it is a question of my being arrested, allow me to wear garters and a tie."

By the time we dressed ourselves, there was no longer anybody in sight. They had disappeared. I roused the servants. Nobody had ever heard of the morals squad. They were mystified. As revealed subsequently, during my divorce from Agnes, it was a most vulgar trick concocted by Hugo-Hugo. Assuming that I might withdraw the confession of my own guilt, Agnes and the baritone, her future husband, and Dr. Hugo-Hugo established, through their paid witnesses, the unquestionable fact of my adultery with Jadviga Jesenska.

The next day I moved with Jadviga Jesenska into my house in the vineyard. The dream cherished by Jadviga Jesenska of finding some rest under a roof that was neither a hotel nor a brothel came true, as did her fear of the pimply stranger with the black tie with white spots. Jadviga was in a way a clairvoyant person, and it was amusing to sip Burgundy in her company, to discuss human stupidity with her, to talk about people being foolish, weak, and essentially unhappy; to listen to the autumnal winds howling around the house, to the flames in the fire, and to Jadviga talking about love and how it was the most flagrant lie of all lies. Only once in her lifetime had she been in love, but even that was silly.

When Dr. Werner was the publisher of *Tribuna,* she was his first wife. It was a long time ago, before the war, when Dr. Werner was in poor financial shape. At that time they lived in a miserable two-room apartment, without any servants; she alone did both the cooking and the sewing, and smoked the cheapest cigarettes. She was in the kitchen frying pancakes when somebody rang the doorbell. It was a twenty-year-old youth. Jadviga knew in advance, after having spotted him through the peephole, that it must be yet another beginner in writing who was bringing manuscripts to her husband, also *Tribuna's* editor-in-chief, a figure in our provincial literary circles. While opening the door to the unidentified young men, she was as cold-blooded as the wives of famous editors of literary gazettes are, the ones frying pancakes and opening the door to beginners in writing.

Unknown young men used to come to her door, bringing their first manuscripts, and through that filthy door they entered into literature, advancing toward glory and fame; they were nervous, their voices trembled. "Promising talents" came and rang the bell, and then carried on with their scribbling, imploring, humiliating themselves like starving dogs, and then in one or two years they themselves became "recognized local figures" and spat at her husband, attacking him as if he were an idiot, even though it was through her door that they began advancing toward glory and it was her husband who had given them a helping hand. Not one of all these men had raised his hat out of courtesy when, later, everybody was saying in bars that she was a nymphomaniac.

"The gentleman is not at home," she politely replied to the young man's question, discreetly glancing at his shoes, which were the most reliable key to the fate of anyone bringing his manuscripts to the editor-in-chief for publication, to launch a new poet, a new genius, yet another desperate man who would end his days like everybody else: on a lecturer's podium, or in an asylum, or on the asphalt pavement as a beggar.

The man's shoes were really torn and the heels run down. He stood in front of her flat-footed, while blue striped socks stained with reddish-brown dye from the wet, old, rotting leather, were sticking out of the patches of his left shoe. It was a rainy autumn, in late October, and that wet creature stood in front of her in his shabby, wrinkled jacket, soaked to the bone, without an umbrella, without an overcoat, reminding her of a drowned man.

"What can this boy be: an elementary-school teacher or an undergraduate?" That was the first thought that crossed Mrs. Werner's mind at the sight of this mysterious man standing in her doorway, a man who was to be the greatest disappointment in her life. In the twilight of the corridor the kettle could be heard murmuring noisily, as if it were out of order. It usually announced itself at the most awkward times, and from the kitchen the smell of melting lard was combined with the frying of pancakes in a baking dish. The fair-haired boy at the door was still a youth with a serene look: a liverwort in bloom illuminated by the sunlight. In rags, with rundown heels, in torn shoes from which rough socks were sticking out, he was a handsome boy, almost incandescent, and a strange, mysterious light emanated from him, as is common with the antiquated varnish in quattrocento temperas: in front of Mrs. Werner a Gabriel stood in a red tunic bordered with gold fringes, announcing good news to her: his heart in hand, with curly blond hair, and, as for his look, a perfect, summer, sunny serenity. It was just for a moment. . . . The reality was of pancakes being fried in the kitchen, an exhausted female body in a fustian dressing-gown standing by an open door to a corridor wrapped in twilight.

The young man appeared to be surprised that Dr. Werner was not at home. It was the twenty-second of October, and he had been told to come for an answer on that particular day. It was a question of his poems, and he was asked to turn up to hear the verdict on the twenty-second. . . .

"I don't know anything about that, young man. Please come back after lunch. At the moment my husband is not in. Good-by."

After closing the door and returning to her pancakes, Mrs. Werner felt really sorry for the young man. He was all wet, almost without shoes, he must have been hungry; why did she not let him into the room to warm himself? Why should she not have offered him the pancakes or lunch? Why should not Werner publish his poems? Overwhelmed by generosity, she rushed to the door to catch the young man on the stairs. But on opening the door once again, she found him still standing there with his head bent, pale-looking, and as handsome as an angel. One could hear the rain pouring down the roofs in the courtyard, the gutters on the roof wailing, everything soaked in October moisture. The young man, when the door was shut before him, realized how shaky and full of fright he was. In his helplessness he was standing in front of the closed door like a beggar. In fear of a deserted street inundated with rushing streams and the rain pouring on the leather roofs of the cabs at the corner, in fear of that fatal October twenty-second when the verdict had to be given as to whether or not he was born to be a poet, the young man remained motionless. When the door opened again and the kind lady in the dark violet dressing-gown invited him to come in, he thought it was a dream. He entered the room of the freethinker, torch- and standard-bearer, Dr. Werner, a room with piles of books in it, statues, pictures, a warm room with an enormous bay window and subtropical plants, and that dear lady asked him to sit down and rest since Dr. Werner was due back any minute now.

He sat down and began to talk to the lady about waiting for more than an hour outside in the rain in front of the window of a toyshop at the corner, next to the two-storied house where the Werners lived. The young man, overcome by fear, contemplated rubber balls, polished steam engines, and a white curly-haired poodle whose muzzle was as red as a clown's. The scent of rubber and polished tin streamed through the open door of the toyshop and encouraged him so that the deep depression burning within him like a hot candle flared into a shining summer heat. He felt the joy of rolling a hoop over the green meadows, the fragrant balls, the red kites, the jigsaw-puzzle pieces that can be used to build an antiquated English port with a gray, misty sky and sailing boats at

anchor at the jetty, with black smoke gushing from the funnel of a
ship sailing at full speed toward Singapore, Borneo, Hawaii. . . .
Cinnamon is sold in those shops in small port towns in England,
constructed of children's puzzle pieces, whole bales of cinnamon,
aromatic spices, pineapples, the moonlight as blue as ink, and a ship
sails to Singapore . . . and thus, standing in the rain, in front of the
toyshop window, he had composed a poem.

If the lady would permit him, he would even read it to her. . . .

That was how Zvonimir Pavlas read his poem to Jadviga Jesenska and that was how on October twenty-second, two or three years
before the war broke out, Dr. Werner discovered Zvonimir Pavlas
as the new hope of our lyrical poetry, and that was how a romance
began, which only fell short of her running away with Pavlas.

"I don't understand. What Pavlas is that?"

"Zvonimir Tihomir Pavlas, the *Gazette* editor."

"I've never heard of Tihomir Pavlas, the *Gazette* editor, as a poet.
Is it the same *Gazette* that carried a piece about our queen's gambit
in one of our most elegant hotels?"

"Yes, that's right. It was that *Gazette*."

"Is it that Tihomir Pavlas who was the first to publish the news
of 'a scandal in the vineyard of a big industrialist'?"

"Yes, it was that Pavlas, the only sincere one-hundred per cent
love of my life. Werner and I accepted him tenderly, almost as a
son. Werner fell in love with him, launched him in spite of everybody, and I dressed him, gave him a bath, patched his clothes, gave
him food, and he moved into our flat. Werner found a job for him
with the *Tribuna* as a technical director. He then began taking examinations and settling down. Werner printed his first book of
poems. I was extremely kind to him. In 1914, when Werner was
arrested, we found out that it was because of Pavlas's denunciation

of him. He was a paid informer in the *Tribuna* editorial board's office. And when, several years ago, I was arrested on account of that cocaine trafficking and when I took cyanide, Pavlas's *Gazette* tormented me during the whole time of the investigation. For a whole week he created a sensation out of my case. People are commonplace swine."

We had not lived in the vineyard for more than a few days when, at daybreak, we were awakened by the infuriated barking of my dog, Lord. Somebody was banging at the glass door to the veranda.

"Who is it?"

"The police!"

"What do you want?"

"Open the door! I've come for registration forms."

It was useless to explain to that gentleman that I was in my own house and that I did not need to register my name and address with the police. But since he displayed more interest in my tenant than in me, I filled in the form and quickly got rid of him. In a few days I was summoned to the office concerned and fined three substantial sums, first for having failed to register myself, secondly for not registering my tenant, and thirdly for having attempted to deceive the authorities by false statements.

I stated that I was a professional doctor of law without any permanent job, a lecher, slanderer, paramour, divorced through my own fault, involved in promiscuity, as established by witnesses. I stated that for the time being I was blameless, but in the remarks column I added, "problematic individual, morally insane."

As for Jadviga, I put: "three times widowed, divorced, without any special occupation, paramour, lives on sale of her own body." In the remarks column I put: "suspected as cocaine trafficker, attempted to commit suicide, punished by ostracism on account of immoral conduct, the first wife of the editor-in-chief Dr. Werner."

In that house of lewdness and madness, lechery, moral corruption, and sin, I lived with Jadviga Jesenska until the trial. She then left for Vienna, and I went to prison for pre-trial confinement.

6

CRIME
AND PUNISHMENT

The courtroom, in which His Honor Dr. Attila von Rugvay opened the trial to pass judgment on me for the quadruple murder by Mr. Domaćinski, was more like a concert hall that day than a courtroom. Everybody was assembled as at a sensational first night at the opera: Sandreta and Pipa, Bobby and Robby, Muki and Kuki, Buki and Cuki, Teddy and Meddy, Baby and Lady, Tekla and Mimi, Madame Dagmar Varagonski with the old lady Aquacurti-Sarvaš-Daljski and the young lady Aquacurti-Mencetić-Maksimirski; in brief: the elite that takes its frozen conservative stand on the unshakable principles underlying the bourgeois way of life, plays bridge perseveringly, kills its boredom by making inane jokes, stages intrigues, makes chamber pots, padlocks, and chains; sells fur and spices; in a nutshell, acts constructively in the interests of the lower classes.

The whole night before this unpleasant trial, I admittedly did not get a wink of sleep. I could not imagine how I could run the gauntlet of those traveling salesmen dealing in neckties, compiling Latin grammars, producing like baboons illegitimate children in the most legitimate marriages, holders of historical titles that were neither historical nor, as titles, anything but a national shame. I have never felt any respect for selfish, promiscuous people or stubborn bachelors who in their mid-sixties marry young girls and then move about in society as respectable cuckolds. Subconsciously they were strangers to me even at times when I mixed with them for business reasons, offering them my so-called professional services. But as I had broken away from that elite by withdrawing into my own solitude, what could that agitated flock of parrots and jays mean to me at the moment when I already saw before me my own flight? Making my appearance at the other end of the courtroom, like a man who shows up late at a concert, I passed through that elite composed of my personal friends, walking on a carpet to a seat in the front row in front of that whole agitated public, which stopped murmuring as soon as the person who was the main attraction at this unique performance made his appearance.

At my place, which in vulgar jargon is called the defendant's bench, I found three copies of the *Gazette*. On the second page, under a sensational headline, "What a Moralist Thinks of Himself," was my photograph and the facsimile of the official report in which I stated that I was a promiscuous person, a slanderer, a paramour, divorced through my own fault, according to witnesses a confirmed adulterer, a problematic man, a morally sick case.

Dr. Attila von Rugvay opened the trial and thereupon, in the name of Mr. Domaćinski, the indictment was read out, bearing the signature of Hugo-Hugo, the Director-General's lawyer, saying that I had declared that Mr. Domaćinski was a bandit, a criminal type of man, a murderer, a born evil-doer, a morally insane type; that he had reached for a revolver and wanted to shoot me, and as I had stated to several persons on various occasions, that Domaćinski was a troublemaker, an adulterer, that he concurrently had illegitimate intercourse with seven women, not to mention his three mistresses. I had alleged that the Director-General Domaćinski had the absolutely certain intention of shooting me like a dog, as he had threatened me with a revolver, etc., etc., so—in view of everything that had been quoted—I had without doubt committed a whole series of criminal deeds against his dignity, according to paragraphs so and so of the Penal Code. . . . Yes, certainly, and so forth, as Dr. Werner would ritually have put it.

With the formalities over, the lawyer of the insulted, slandered and humiliated Director-General Domaćinski, Dr. Hugo-Hugo, took the floor.

To influence the court and the public by producing contrasts, so as to depict in high relief all the moral corruption and malicious perfidiousness of my behavior, Dr. Hugo-Hugo, a brilliant orator with long practice, first outlined the portrait of an injured person.

"Only in the light of the marked and dominant profile of that distinguished representative of our elite can one, Honorable Court, create a correct and true picture of the incredibly destructive effect of those slanders, insinuations, and defamations so logically defined by our Penal Code. *Jus est ars boni et aequi*—the law is a balance between goodness and harmony, the law is a perfect accord between taste and convictions. For this reason, this obscure and profoundly insane case should be examined with the calm that is due matters on which verdicts are to be pronounced in the name of morality, in the name of human dignity, in the name of the ideal that rules time and space and is called justice.

"Who is the slandered and injured Domaćinski? He is one of the most distinguished and highly reputable dignitaries in our national economy, one of the far-sighted founders and clairvoyant managers, governors, and architects of the foundation that is, in the contemporary competition of material forces, a prerequisite of every national economy, and this is our hope, our sole justification for existence in the economic sense—our domestic industry. You see that gray-haired worker, that gentleman whose sixtieth birthday was recently celebrated by all the institutions, corporations, and outstanding bodies of our diversified public body, that most deserving among all the celebrators and simultaneously the most modest among them, who is not only an inspired and enthusiastic creator of material assets but is also, as an outstanding figure, a national benefactor, author of good deeds, in fact a patron commanding nationwide gratitude: *aere perennius,* full of good deeds and charitable activity, unprecedented in the annals of our more recent past, that exemplary and significant figure, meritorious public worker and pioneer, not only in the field of the cooperative movement, finance, industry and commerce, but also, in general, a pioneer of planned, systematic, managerial organization in our young economy. This great man had the experience one day of being spat on, insulted, and slandered by a man who described himself in an official, practically public statement 'as a problematic and morally insane individual.'

"The deeds, life work, constructive, altruistic achievements of the Director-General Domaćinski are before us. They have been visible to all contemporaries and to all his collaborators, both in the broader and in the narrower sense, for the last two decades. These constructive achievements may be criticized like every other creative

work of man and, if judged in the light of malice or envy, may even
have some barely discernible shortcomings, but there is not a single
man throughout our vast and beautiful homeland who, as an
impartial observer of this magnificent endeavor, would not be
prompted to bow to the man who achieved all those wonderful results. Honorable Court, cast even the most careless glance at the
sawmills, at the electric power plants, at the turbines, at those trains
loaded with hides, ties, boards sent daily across our borders and thus
raising the value of our own currency—consequently of our own
standard of living. Just look, please, at those coal mines, the ships,
the shopwindows displaying a great variety of goods, and ask whose
achievement all this is and who should be given credit for its existence in our country, where practically ten or twenty years earlier
there was nothing. It is the achievement of a single lonely individual—a man like Domaćinski, who is by our standards a kind of
superman, an idealist who deals with economics not out of egotistic
motives, but in the higher, architectural sense, prompted by pure
creativity, motivated by the human impulse that has through the
centuries raised all epochs of man to a higher level. Such a man
must not be spat on, slandered, smeared, without being given on
behalf of all of us the satisfaction that such a generous idealist is
fully justified in expecting: satisfaction in the form of rigid and
just punishment.

"For, Honorable Court, addressing today this esteemed forum,
devoid of every feeling that is ignoble, I must draw your attention
to the terrible allegations raised by the defendant, and, however
vague and undefined they are, they have not and could not have any
deeper meaning but to depict the plaintiff as a selfish and greedy
animal shooting innocent people like mad dogs, threatening his own
guests with a loaded revolver, amassing earthly riches out of innate,
insatiable greed, wallowing in the mud and stink of his own family

life due to a primordial moral blindness that is the symbol of egoism and criminality.

"What egoism can be detected in the life work of Domaćinski?
We have all, as high school students, when studying the elementary
works of logic, learned that man is mortal and, as Domaćinski is
just a man, he, too, is therefore mortal and, like the commonest
mortal he, too, will eventually deliver his earthly belongings into
the hands of the One placed above all courts and judging all judg-
ments. Domaćinski, too, will therefore one day close his earthly
eyes, but he will not die altogether because his deeds will preserve
his memory. The achievements he has bequeathed to us will belong
to future generations of our people. Domaćinski as a representative
of our generous type of man ranks among the most disinterested
creators of material assets. Domaćinski has developed towns, along
with roads, institutions, hydroelectric power plants, the electric network, the press, poorhouses, machines. He is the founder of charitable and educational institutions; he is the guardian of our poor
and illiterate proletariat; in fact, he has raised the lowest stratum of
our people to a higher level; he has shouldered his heavy burden
of responsibility vigilantly and sublimely; he has guarded our national interests like a watchdog of both consciousness and conscience; he is a patriot in that higher sense that has so often been
abused; he does not lament over national worries, fully aware that
in life success is achieved only through a thorough, strenuous effort
of both the will and the intelligence. Knowing perfectly well that
sympathy for national interests does not mean empty and meddle-
some talk but work, doing it silently according to a serious and
noble plan, that philanthropist who helps the poor, that founder of
public kitchens, baths, and recreational centers for children, that
gentleman, in the genuine sense of the word, on one particular day

was spat at, insulted, and even slandered as an assassin, a criminal, a morally corrupt phenomenon.

"Esteemed Court, the righteous man is not great in the eyes of God because he plays the role of a purist in life, but for having left behind good deeds after his life is done. And the graying representative of our most distinguished elite did not become gray-haired through loafing, did not marry any medicinal tea producer's daughter [laughter in court]; he did not pretend over the years to be a common lackey who would eventually spit on his benefactor and employer; that excellent, militant man, that unique champion of merit and virtue, that simple and good man, whatever he has earned, he has earned decently through his own work and talent. So, logically, he is fully entitled to seek satisfaction from society, the organized national community.

"Domaćinski ranks among those wise and experienced public workers in our country who have never been involved in petty politicking. Domaćinski has never considered cunning as an aim of politics. In his view, his economic mission has always been something placed above daily political considerations. He believes that a real people's teacher can only be the individual who has made up his mind to act as the people's servant. That selfless founder of more than two hundred eleven diverse societies, that sponsor of the most reputable national and patriotic foundations, honorary citizen of nearly all our free towns and trading centers, that man who for more than forty years has been perseveringly and unshakably acting along the lines of a national guardian, that outstanding champion striving for the strengthening of the national economy, a modest and pious believer, a good patriot, an exemplary and sincere donor of numerous places of worship in our town and in the provinces, a man who certainly did no harm to anybody, who, so to say, has never killed a fly, does such a man—with such a record of public life that is very well known to us—deserve to be told that he is a born criminal, a criminal type of man, and a murderer?

"I ask you, Honorable Court, how could that mentor who has helped so many thousands of our outstanding toilers, that most prominent and persistent and diligent worker within the framework of his own enterprises, that son of our country born in the Zagorje, a citizen of Zagreb, a Croat, a Slav, a Yugoslav, a Pan-Slav, a European, that man who was thrown out of the civil service by the foreign authorities because of his political convictions, that fine gentleman known far and wide beyond the boundaries of our homeland —how could such a man threaten someone with a revolver?

"Thousands and thousands of guests have been invited to the house of this most hospitable host; whole processions of people have over the years been treated at his rich table; thousands of people have been sustained through his generosity; his life's work will be the unforgettable pride of a whole nation, and who can dare denounce that good-humored donor, that man who welcomes everybody with outstretched arms, that model Christian, as a criminal type, a criminal and murderer?

"And why? Yes, Honorable Court, we raise this logical question in order to examine all the circumstances that have brought us into this thankless situation of dealing with a sad episode from our distant political past that should have rather remained buried under the veil of oblivion.

"Why? Because twenty years ago, during a stormy night, he fired at burglars? Honorable Court, as this, in itself a tragic and pathetic event, is the only fact indicating that the case should, without doubt, be judged according to Paragraph two hundred ninety-eight of the Penal Code, consisting of a whole series of criminal offenses against human dignity, as an advocate of the plaintiff's interests, I am

obliged, Honorable Court, to call your attention to the special circumstances under which that tragedy occurred. In fact, amid the
universal anarchy of 1918, it was a question of a most ordinary burglary, an incursion by armed, masked robbers, of an attack not only
against other people's property but on actual life, which had to be
resisted in the best way, in the only way one knew.

"According to Paragraph twenty-four of the Penal Code, an act
of crucial self-defense is far from being unlawful. It is both justified
and logical, and every citizen is entitled to resist an unlawful assault. Is that kind of protection against unlawful assault a crime,
and has the individual gone beyond the limits of his own crucial defense, by firing at common, masked, armed burglars at night, in the
fall, when it was pitch-dark, after having been fired at by a rifle?

"That exceptional situation, Honorable Court, when the en-
raged, brutalized masses set fire to, robbed and destroyed everything that came within their reach, that awful state of anarchy when
blood was shed in streams, that highly tense, revolutionary, yes, indeed revolting revolutionary situation, was in itself pregnant with
the possibility, in fact not only the possibility but rather the right
and authority, or even more than that: the duty of restoring civil
order and a lawful system. Whoever might have committed any
act of restoring civil order in those sad, terrible, criminal conditions
cannot by any moral criterion be declared guilty, but just the opposite: such an individual was at that moment, and is still to this day,
meritorious in the eyes of his people and his homeland. Had we,
Honorable Court, in the days of both national and social chaos had
the luck to have several dozen Domaćinskis, the infuriating and
blind anarchy of those days would not have taken us to the impasse
in which we landed in 1918. According to what logic and morality
should we be permitted now to spit publicly in the face of a man
who at the time of national catastrophe possessed so much moral

courage as to struggle with rifle in hand for the national and social ideals in those days when nearly the whole intelligentsia in our country was lulled by its passive, quasi-progressive dream, as it is even today, when under the influence of current events in the world such morally unstable individuals, like the accused, fly off the handle."

Applause in court.

"Plaudite, cives," I thought, listening to the loud applause in the middle of the scene, for by that time there could be no doubt that the sympathies of the public in the courtroom were on the side of the plaintiff, on the side of his brilliant lawyer, and that the pro-longed and demonstrative applause in fact concerned me, seated in the front bench, at the head of the class. Once again I had failed to learn the lesson.

Why did Hugo-Hugo learn the lesson, why has Hugo-Hugo al-ways learned the lesson, why is Hugo-Hugo always ready while you helplessly sweat on the front bench, rustle a newspaper, read the article by Tihomir Pavlas about yourself, about your moral cor-ruption, and once again you are not ready, once again you are going to be questioned, and again you will not know what to say in reply . . . ?

Well, of course Hugo-Hugo is an excellent student, Hugo-Hugo is a grind, Hugo-Hugo is a hustler, Hugo-Hugo will pass his exami-nations with high marks, Hugo-Hugo will receive the king's ring as a gift in token of the highest recognition by His Imperial and Royal Majesty Franz Josef I, Hugo-Hugo will be promoted *sub auspiciis regis,* Hugo-Hugo will become the most outstanding orator in the whole legal profession, Hugo-Hugo will make a vast profit out of this phonographic record of his (which he played to the satisfaction of the whole public in the courtroom), Hugo-Hugo will also charge

me, too, for his lawyer's fees, Hugo-Hugo is the master of the situation and has a great sense of humor; he is making a fool of me, he
is exposing me to ridicule for having forced myself on a druggist's
fat daughter because her dowry consisted of profit from digestive tea,
but, to tell the truth, I can't learn anything by heart, I've never been
able to do so, if something was not clear to me. And, honestly, all
this is not in the least clear to me. . . .

The machine-gun of Dr. Hugo-Hugo was thundering and dis-
charging its superlatives on and on at the tireless, accurate, mathe-
matically calculated speed of a correctly leveled, solid, perfectly
equipped machine that aimed at my irreproachable conduct, fired
at me with such accuracy that around my head evidence exploded
with such fatal conviction that I could hear amid that torrent of
moral shots the clinking of the spent shells of phrases used by
Hugo-Hugo. The sharp proofs of Hugo-Hugo's shots whistled,
every one of which could destroy my single, miserable and even to
some extent ridiculous argument that in this case, when I reacted to
Domaćinski's move, as far as I was concerned it was not the question of the objective, civil, external dignity of that unquestionably
reputable man but of the human, internal, invisible notion of honor.
In that case, well, yes, certainly, but, and so forth. . . .

Hugo-Hugo, a robot megaphone in lawyer's robes, thundered before the high forum that Domaćinski was the organizer of our
mountaineering, tourism, agriculture, the tanners' profession; Domaćinski was a high official in all our cultural institutions; Domaćinski was the chairman in the society for the advancement of our science; Domaćinski was a plowman in the pleiades of our economy,
which has produced such celebrities as Sikirica, Milanović, Petrano-
vić, Jarac, etc., etc.; Domaćinski was the holder of the highest decorations awarded by the Emperor and the King; Domaćinski laid the
foundations of a bank that treats even the smallest shareholders on

an equal footing with the biggest ones; Domaćinski was the re-
organizer of the banking system on contemporary, humanitarian
lines; Domaćinski was from an old family, one of us, arbiter of
taste, a name that will be connected with the flourishing of our industry for a whole eternity, a wise helmsman for our most humble
depositors; Domaćinski was a big land owner; Domaćinski was an
economist; Domaćinski was a model vintner; a pioneer in automo-
biling; Domaćinski was a champion of the most elementary prerequisites of our economy; Domaćinski was a realist; Domaćinski
was the protagonist of national dignity abroad, before the large
commercial, industrial, and banking forums where, in the realm of
international commissions, national dignity is defended in terms of
arguments different from the ones imagined by a semi-educated and
backward provincial intelligentsia drinking wine on the veranda,
who hope to be able to divert such an intellect of broad horizons as
Domaćinski from his creative road by means of lies and disgusting
intrigues. Is a Domaćinski, the initiator of so many grandiose under-
takings, that spirit as energetic as a whirlwind, the man whose place
in the history of our economy has been guaranteed, that gigantic,
diverse, and monumental creator of magnificent achievements, that
important man who despised nothing in the world more than empty
talk, is such a Domaćinski to be confused or misled by empty talk
from a nameless, puzzled, confused employee who declares that he
is a promiscuous and adulterous man himself, who associates in public with publicly and notoriously promiscuous women without even
being ashamed of it?

Without any properly built umbrella to ward off that pouring
rain, hit by that elemental outpouring of phrases, I felt that the fantastic superlatives were carrying me along on a dangerous torrent; I
saw that cataract of lies and folly, that waterfall of rhetoric drawing

me to itself with a practically irresistible power. I was unscrupulously unmasked by Dr. Hugo-Hugo and reduced to the significance I had always had within the confines of that society (the insignificant dimensions of a hired employee), naked and despised as a confirmed adulterer and slanderer; I sensed the urgent and not particularly honorable imminent sinking of myself and my small rubber boat. I felt I was swimming on and on, carried by muddy water, dragged toward an enormous cataract of illogic, prejudices, public opinion, legal implications, while over there, in the distance, the prince's regatta, magnificent with the fluttering of its victorious flags and purple sails, a whole fleet of superlatives about Domaćinski, was sailing: Domaćinski the admiral, Domaćinski the Lord Protector; his ships loaded with tin washbowls and chamber pots bound for Persia; his trains loaded with the most varied goods; his banks, towns, flashing neon signs—Domaćinski Cherry Brandy, Domaćinski soap, smokestacks, the steamship smoke, the engine smoke, the smoke gushing from the huge workshops, the clanking of the machines, transmission belts, the blowing of horns, the press, the newspapers, the special issue of the *Gazette*—the Domaćinski affair in court, the slanderer sentenced to eight months' imprisonment at hard labor, a special issue, Domaćinski—Dr. Hugo-Hugo—Domaćinski. . . .

It was a criminal act against dignity—because I undoubtedly "insulted someone"—punishable by a prison term of up to one year or a fine of up to ten thousand. The least evil would be to be fined a sum up to ten thousand by Von Rugvay, but he is a nephew of Madame Aquacurti-Sarvaš-Daljski, and he would not fine me but would give me a prison sentence. As the kind of punishment depends on his discretion, he will, beyond all doubt, sentence me to at least eight months' imprisonment, and, in line with his free choice, deprive me of freedom of movement. . . .

With reference to Domaćinski, I had declared that he was a murderer, a bandit, a criminal type, a morally insane person, that he
wanted to shoot me, that he had reached for his revolver and was
prevented from shooting only at the very last moment; I had unquestionably assailed the dignity of the other man; I had undoubtedly stated that I did not respect the other man sufficiently, that is,
Director-General Domaćinski, and now this could not be denied;
this state of affairs should be faced directly. In this case one should
nevertheless be more or less consistent. This was no longer a private
conversation, a conversation with individual people; it was a game
before the green desk, before Von Rugvay, seated on the other side
of a nickel crucifix with his cold, penetrating, fishy look sliding
down my body like an eel, sniffing away, his pince-nez glittering behind the nickel crucifix on which a Christ made of yellow brass was
hanging, though I could not see the Christ, only his arms forming a
triangle reflected on the crucifix: two dark strokes against the clear
white light entering the warm, crowded room through the window.
Galoshes, perfumes, women, tar, coal. In heavy, vertical, watery
flakes the wet snow was falling outside. A pigeon flew by the window and the fluttering of the wings could be heard inside the courtroom, where Dr. Hugo-Hugo was still howling about Domaćinski.
Outside, spring was in the air. It was a foggy February, the gutters
were singing, one could hear the girls laughing in the street, and
from a high poplar, full of yellow rotted leaves, the shaking off of
a patch of wet snow was accompanied by the terrified twittering of
the sparrows, which dispersed in all directions among the branches
like black bits of shrapnel after an explosion.

Dr. Hugo-Hugo said that the target of my attack was beyond discussion a public figure. According to paragraph 297, it is punishable
if someone insults another individual. Yes, of course. But, according

to paragraph 298, if someone incites somebody else to hurt him by his improper conduct or a criminal act. . . .

Was I not provoked by the improper behavior of that troglodyte? Undoubtedly.

My insult was a logical consequence of the conduct by the plaintiff. For, firstly, he had killed, and secondly he had been boasting of a quadruple murder.

The insult therefore followed a provocation, a moral one, to be sure, but nevertheless a provocation. And the case could also be interpreted according to paragraph 311: if the accused "provides evidence of the truthfulness of his statement, he will not be punished as a slanderer, but he may be sentenced for the insult." Domaćinski wanted to shoot me like a dog. He declared that he would shoot me like a dog, and that he regretted not having shot me like a dog. He really reached for his revolver to shoot me like a dog. This can be proved by witnesses. . . .

Which witnesses?

Our highly learned, important figures, aristocrats, our dear, beloved, and truthful neighbors . . . as witnesses? There was no need to tell the truth at that moment. . . . It was not opportune. . . . It was far more intelligent to shut up, like a dog. . . .

That was the standpoint of my wife Agnes, of Minister Mark Antony Javoršek, the Minister of Postage Stamps Mr. Harambašević, that was the "Yes, certainly, of course, and so on and so forth" stand of Dr. Werner; that was the doggish stand of "in general and in particular" of gentlefolk like Dr. Hugo-Hugo, Von Rugvay, Madame Aquacurti-Daljski, that is what I thought until I was fifty-two, and what practical use is it to stop thinking along such ingrained lines?

Of course, I cannot provide evidence to show that Domaćinski really intended to shoot me. I cannot prove that he actually reached for his revolver. I can prove nothing at all as regards Domaćinski because he is not a man, an individual. He is an abstraction—a symbol of social conditions and relations, and what sense is there in arguing with guns, arsenals, steamships, funnels, patent nails and tin chamber pots exported to Persia? According to paragraph 300, I will, "beyond any discussion," according to Dr. Hugo-Hugo, "be punished." "Whoever with the intention of exposing somebody to contempt accuses him of a criminal deed though the latter may have been sentenced for that reason, or tells this to somebody else, even though a verdict had already been pronounced and the sentence served, out-of-date, commuted or expired, is liable to a prison sentence of up to six months or to a fine of up to five thousand. . . ."

With the intention of exposing Domaćinski to contempt, I accused him of a criminal deed; and that criminal deed was not criminal at all, since it was a glorious achievement for which he is meritorious before the people, future generations, the whole homeland; during that stormy night he was really a prophet predicting the trend European politics was to pursue, and that was why no verdict was passed and he did not serve any sentence whatever, because he was not guilty at all, and nevertheless I accused him of something that did not exist, and that was why I would be punished—according to paragraph 300.

One is not allowed to accuse anyone even of a committed deed, as it is an obvious sign of social intolerance, and it is especially intolerant socially if one man accuses another of a crime that in reality is an exploit, something of historical significance. When it is punishable by law to accuse someone of being a criminal, how can one punish someone accusing somebody else of a chivalrous deed, of a heroic exploit, of an ethical gesture, of a deed restoring social order in the struggle against anarchy? I am undoubtedly also to be pun-

ished according to paragraph 301: "Whoever says or rumors something that is not true, something that may harm the dignity, good
reputation, or economic credit of another person will be imprisoned.
If the slanderer did this with the special purpose in mind of ruining
the other person's good reputation or economic credit, he will be
punished severely, up to at least six months' imprisonment." . . .
Slander is an untruth, slandering harms man's dignity, good reputation, economic credit, and as Domaćinski is by no means a quadruple murderer who regrets not having killed the fifth man, i.e., not
having killed me too, as Domaćinski is not a criminal type of man
but a builder of the national road, a patron of our economy and so
forth, therefore that untruth that he really wanted to kill me like a
dog and that he had reached for a revolver to shoot me like a dog
may harm his unquestionably good name, his dignity and repute,
giving the impression that he really wanted to kill me like a dog
but actually did not do it. My destructive endeavors undoubtedly
betray a tendency to undermine his honor, his good reputation, his
economic credit, good repute, and so forth. Yes, of course, but, and
so forth . . . and therefore I would be punished as I deserve, and it
would be a tangible punishment, an exemplary one. It would serve
me right. Why had I taken a seat at that wretched lawyer's table
with Dr. Hugo-Hugo if I did not know how to play the game?

The hellish machine gun of Dr. Hugo-Hugo rat-a-tatted on:
Domaćinski, Domaćinski, Domaćinski, economy, name, good reputation, heroism, ethics, anarchy, paragraph, paragraph, paragraph so
and so, Domaćinski, paragraph, generosity, humanism, *dolus even-
tualis, animus iniurandi, Beleidigung, offensio, Verleumdung, calumnia, delictum sui generis, la vie privée doit être murée, animus
laedendi, Schmähung, ratio legis, delictum continuatum,* defamation,
slandering, dignity, Domaćinski, the law, the paragraphs, more
paragraphs, Domaćinski. Listening to that law machine spewing

forth evidence at such a convincing speed that the whole courtroom was inundated with proofs, arguments, paragraphs, and
around me on the defendant's bench such a mass of slanders, crimes,
offenses, criminal deeds, lies, insults, cheating, untruths, crimes,
moral insanity, malice, moral misery, I began to feel myself disappearing under the strokes of that gravedigger's shovel, being buried
in the grave formed by my own moral rottenness, the clods of justice dropped on my miserable coffin, boom-boom, one following the
other, increasingly heavy each time, boom-boom-boom, so that I
could breathe only with more and more difficulty; under that pressure I was gradually getting lost in a labyrinth of my own truly
revolting moral doom; I saw that I was sinking into the mud. I
watched the sky. High above the poplars it was gray, grayer and
grayer, the snowflakes were getting thicker and thicker, everything
was increasingly monotonous, straight vertical lines formed quickly,
the courtroom began to travel upwards faster and faster, like an elevator. I was traveling. In the distance bells were chiming in the
town, and next to me a sewing machine was making a burial gar-
ment for me, tra-ta, tra-ta-tra-ta, pa-ra-graphs, tra-ta-tra-ta. Everything was so tedious, that perfume in the courtroom, that Madame
Aquacurti, Hugo-Hugo, Domaćinski—*delictum continuatum, la vie
privée.* . . .

"Hello, hello, Doctor! It seems that your conscience is so clear
you can fall asleep on the defendant's bench. Will you behave properly, because otherwise I am going to be compelled to remind you
in a disciplinary fashion of your duties. What kind of democratic
conduct is that?"

Laughter in court.

I was awakened by the voice of Dr. Attila von Rugvay, and I
raised my head: "I beg your pardon?"

Laughter in court.

"Don't you beg me anything here. What are you 'begging' of me? We are in court, Doctor. One does not sleep in court."

"What do you want?"

"What do I want? Ahem. I ask you for the third time whether you have anything to reply to the statement by plaintiff's attorney? Please pull yourself together. This is not a school where you may just sit back on your bench. It is not proper conduct for a mature person."

Loud laughter resounding in the whole court brought me to my senses.

"Oh, yes. *Diffamatio, ratio legis, calumnia,* Hugo-Hugo, Doma-ćinski. I beg your pardon, I'm not trying to prove anything. I am at your disposal. What can I do for you?"

"Well, Doctor, I don't understand you. Have you some idea of getting out of this whole affair through mental incompetence? Perhaps you think that, according to paragraph two hundred fifty-three of the Criminal Proceedings, I should invite a psychiatrist?"

Laughter in court.

"Why a psychiatrist? If a person is bored, it does not mean that he needs a psychiatrist. Please carry on. . . ."

"Are you going to answer the speech of the plaintiff's attorney? I ask you this question for the last time. No jokes, please, Remember that. Stand up while you are talking to me."

In point of fact, up to that moment I really had absolutely no intention of speaking. If that odious Attila von Rugvay had not been acting as chief magistrate, it is more than probable that I would have stuck to my original decision: to say not a word in reply; to acknowledge the verdict; to express satisfaction at the punishment pronounced without protest. In brief, to play the passive role of a dullard who pleads guilty but does not feel, in spite of his statement of guilt, that he is guilty in fact. But that Attila von

Rugvay, from the other side of the crucifix and the green cloth, that son of Arpad von Rugvay, vice-president of the Hungarian Club and chairman of the profitable railway company (who as Khuen's representative at the general election ordered twenty-seven voters to be shot so as to secure for himself a safe majority as prescribed by law), that Arpad's Attila whom I had rebuffed less than six months earlier as the suitor of my eldest daughter, that aristocrat did, I admit, disturb me by his presence from the very start. I could have requested he be disqualified from conducting the trial, according to paragraphs 28 and 31 of the Criminal Proceedings, since he had asked for my daughter's hand together with the three-storied house at Bishop Square and I had refused to give him either her or the house, because of my personal dislike for him in the first place and, secondly, because I did not want my grandchildren to be the children of an Attila, or even less, the grandchildren of an Arpad. I asked my eldest daughter how things stood with that Attila von Rugvay, whether it was a question of a "romance" or something of that kind; but the child (socially limited, by the way, like her mother) was absolutely passive in reply to my question. "It is a question of the three-storied house and not of any love affair." That is what she said, adding that she despised his "type." If Dr. von Rugvay had not exposed me to the ridicule of the whole distinguished court (which he was right in doing to some extent, because I had really fallen asleep for a moment during Hugo-Hugo's tirade), if he had not then obviously provoked me by his malicious remark that I wanted to evade responsibility by pretending to be an insane sleepy head unaware of the consequences of his behavior, I would not have opposed anything. Ground very fine by the babbling of Domaćinski's attorney, turned into a loose handful of judicial ashes, I would have consented to be scattered to the four winds and to having my earthly ashes used to blot the sentence signed with the thick ink of human folly in which I was sinking like a worn-out fly in an inkpot. The laughter with which I was honored by the distinguished court was completely immaterial to me. I felt superior to that distinguished mob, to that selected trash, just as apes in a zoo do while watching mankind grinning and grimacing on the other side of the cage. But when Attila von Rugvay mockingly pulled me by the ear as if he were really dealing with an idiot, when he began to talk to me as if addressing a brutalized piece of meat hanging from a madman's railing in an asylum, then to his tone—like that of a schoolmaster—I responded in my turn with spite. That this short-sighted, pimply face, with the ash-gray necktie with its white spots like the tail of a guinea fowl, should be treating me like a cretin, appeared to me at the time as being below my sense of dignity. I have never enjoyed jumping from high-diving boards, but at that moment I threw myself from the fifty-second level of my life's experience as if I had three parachutes in each of my pockets.

Under the protection of paragraph 229 of the Criminal Proceedings, Mr. Attila von Rugvay urged me energetically and loudly, this time in the tone of an insulted officer, to get out of my seat.

"Stand up! You must answer standing. Do you understand? I must warn you that you must not disturb the order of the proceedings by your improper conduct. Do you understand what I have been telling you?"

"I beg your pardon?"

"I am asking you if you understand the indictment?"

"Yes, I do."

"Do you plead guilty?"

"I admit that I have talked like that, as is stated in the indictment and as Dr. Hugo-Hugo more or less neatly and clearly stated, but I do not plead guilty."

"Well now, what's this? Are you going to answer the questions? Yes or no?"

Laughter in court.

"Well, go on. Here we are. Do you hear me? The public is laughing at you."

Vox populi, vox dei. That is what I had in mind, but said aloud: "It doesn't matter. It's all right."

Laughter in court.

"I must warn you once again to behave properly, otherwise I shall be compelled to punish you according to disciplinary rules. Do you understand me? It's up to you now to speak. Please do."

"If it is a must, very well. To adhere to the style of the preceding speaker, I, too, shall begin with a quotation from the classics. For instance: *lex est quod notamus.*"

"What do you mean?" Attila von Rugvay interrupted me after my first sentence, under the protection of imperial paragraph 229. "Are you leveling your words at the law in general?"

"No, I just had in mind the logic of the preceding speaker, Your Honor. Dr. Hugo-Hugo imagines that what Hugo the notary puts down must be law itself. This is what I had in mind and that is how I put it: *lex est quod notamus.* But what Dr. Hugo-Hugo puts down need not be a law for me. I appreciate Seneca far more than the logic of a notary like the gentleman acting as his plaintiff's attorney. In fact, while lamenting Pompey, he very intelligently supposed that even underneath Pompey's toga his drawers were not always perfectly clean. . . . *Magni nominis umbra.* . . . The shade of even the greatest name always remains just a shade. However miserable I may seem to myself at this moment, indeed really worthy of sympathy, I have never thought that in my own court case I would speak so pathetically about togas, and practically in hexameter. And insofar as the superb speech by the preceding speaker, Dr. Hugo-Hugo, in his capacity of Director-General Domaćinski's attorney, can be criticized at all from its formal aspect, one could only make the reproach that the magnificent and in every respect imposing poem was not composed in verse. Dithyrambs should absolutely be in verse. . . .

"Mr. Hugo-Hugo has painted such a fine portrait of a patrician that I trust there is not a single individual in this courtroom who has not a clear picture of that great man, Mr. Domaćinski. A phenomenon, it could be said, of unquestionable historical significance. . . .

"We have heard who that gentleman called Domaćinski is. He is a bank director-general, an engineer, a jubilee celebrator, an idealist, a realist, an altruist, a patron, a mentor and protector, a donor and protector. As a worker, he is the best among the best, president and co-founder of several hundreds of societies, the people's tribune, servant and teacher, the people's protector in matters of national dignity and of the national well-being; he is a great man among outstanding people; a pleiad among pleiades; and once again—may I repeat it for the thirty-third time—an idealist, a realist, an altruist, mentor and lord protector, he is the most hospitable host, a model Christian, organizer of the mountaineering movement, and one of us. I don't know whether on this earth there is an illiterate or an uneducated person who could doubt, after such a convincing speech by the most honorable preceding speaker, that Mr. Domaćinski is not one of us, or that in our country there are not many people like him. Is there such an ignoramus who does not know . . ."

"I must warn you, Doctor, that this is not the point. Will you stick to the subject, please."

"If 'stick to the subject' means that I am not going to be given an opportunity even to end my first sentence, I think that the whole game becomes pointless."

"What has been going on here is no 'game,' do you understand me? I am not here to listen to your witty talk, is that clear? First you fall asleep and then make irresponsible provocations. This is my last warning. Deal with the matter, stick to the subject; it's your turn."

"You say that you have given me the floor for the second time, but in fact you've interrupted me for the second time, and now it's not my turn at all. How else can one weigh before this esteemed forum the skill of my oration in comparison with the verbosity of the preceding speaker without it being permitted that I, too, deal with the personality of the injured and slandered plaintiff? For myself, in my own defense, I cannot say pathetically that I am 'a graying jubilee celebrator,' or that I am 'a patron,' 'an idealist' or 'protector,' since I've never favored anybody and have never celebrated any jubilee. It's a pity, but it is true. Thus, I have no 'jubilee' to celebrate, and Domaćinski has, as Dr. Hugo-Hugo said. He is in fact celebrating 'a jubilee.' I'm not 'a bank director-general,' 'engineer,' or 'factory owner,' and Domaćinski is both 'an engineer' and 'a bank director,' but he is not a doctor of law as I am. And what can be proved by saying that he is something that I am not, or that I am not something that he is—for instance, that he is a model patriot, the organizer of the mountaineering movement, the most hospitable host who threatens his guests with a revolver, declaring that he was sorry for not killing them all like dogs, or that he would kill them one and all like dogs?"

"That's not true. Domaćinski never told you anything like that! It is one of your conscious untruths. It belongs to the vicious circle of your fantasy," Dr. Hugo-Hugo irritably interrupted.

"All right. After listening to you for more than two full hours so silently that I even fell asleep—violating the rules of conduct in this eminent institution—there is no doubt that I deserve, on your part at least, to be treated in the same way. You sleep peacefully, I won't worry about it, but please take it into consideration that I am talking to you without anybody's protection. You are not going to persuade me to change my mind by shouting me down. I do not intend to take back a single word I've said: *nescit vox missa reverti.* I stick to every word I have stated. I only want to explain how it came about that I made those statements of mine at all and how it happens that I unconditionally insist on not giving up a single one of my statements, and this is in fact what I have been prevented from doing on both sides."

"What both sides?" Dr. Attila von Rugvay yelled at me as if I were a thief. "What do you mean by both sides?"

"On the part of the esteemed High Court and on the part of the honorable plaintiff, equally."

"It would be much wiser to stick to the subject."

"Very well, let's stick to the subject. The subject is reflected in the indictment for criminal acts against dignity by insult under paragraph two hundred ninety-seven of the Penal Code, paragraph three hundred of the Penal Code, and slander under paragraph three hundred one of the Penal Code, and I am sticking to that subject. All right. The indictment is defended by Dr. Hugo-Hugo, and I am my own defense attorney. To explain those insults and slanders by the accused, I must deal with the personality of the slandered and insulted plaintiff. For why should the accused insult the plaintiff if, as it seems, he had no reason for doing so? We've heard from the lawyer of the insulted and slandered plaintiff that the insulted and slandered plaintiff is a synthesis of seventy-seven thousand descriptive adjectives, so, if I understand it properly, Mr. Domaćinski, in the flesh, is nothing but one magnificent *epiteton ornans* who has only seemingly assumed the shape of an ordinary man, but is in reality a mysterious creature, a platonic dream of an ideal superman: 'good,' 'modest,' 'benefactor,' 'pious,' 'orthodox,' 'altar constructor,' 'church donor,' 'an altruist,' 'a patron,' etc. . . . This praiseworthy effort by Dr. Hugo-Hugo to depict the objective, external, civil honor of an injured person deserves another, far better and more appropriate reply than that which this gentleman acting for the accused has been performing, namely, to prove something that has never been denied by anyone. I've never been interested in the question of the external, civic dignity of Mr. Domaćinski. . . . Have I ever said that Mr. Domaćinski was not an industrialist, a jubilee celebrator, that he was not the co-founder of two hundred eleven societies?"

"Ridiculous. It is more than three months since you've been trumpeting *urbi et orbi* that Domaćinski is a criminal type of man."

"Is that so? And you think that the fact that a person is 'co-founder of two hundred eleven societies' excludes the possibility of such 'a co-founder of two hundred eleven societies' killing four men for a liter of Riesling and that he boasts of a quadruple murder? For a whole two hours you've been—admittedly, in a rather naive fashion—talking about the entirely unimportant aspects of the 'objective,' 'external,' 'decorative,' 'civic' dignity of a man, which are indisputable, because what you've been stating as real has not been denied by the accused. But what the defendant has said to be beyond discussion is a statement by the insulted and slandered Mr. Director-General Domaćinski: that he killed four men like four dogs, and that he was sorry not to have killed the accused like a fifth dog. And why? Because the defendant—without any *animus iniurandi*—dared to remark that it was morally insane to boast of a quadruple murder. What in this concrete case can be the components of 'ex-

ternal honor or the dignity of man as such'? The fact that somebody
shoots superlatives from his lawyer's position like a machine gun
and levels them against the accused as if conducting an examination, that he makes himself highly important by speaking about the
honor of the profession and the civic functions of his client, his
pride in his credits, his reputation, the firemen's brigades who play
serenades to that client, about the fact that the wife of that client
sponsored this or that banner or award, or that the client had had
three altars built—all this is not only unimportant in the examination of this case but has absolutely nothing to do with it.

"Following nothing but common sense, I have denied the inner
human dignity of a murderer; I have dared to establish that that
man has a fatal, insane lack of inborn sense of good taste: after his
statement that he 'shot four men like four dogs,' I declared that a
normal and more or less decent person would not boast of it, that
is, of having shot four men 'like four dogs' for a liter of Riesling. I
did not reproach him with a single word for having killed, but for
considering that bloody murder as an honorable experience that one
can boast of to one's guests. On this matter, that is, the question of
good taste, I differ in essence, on principle, and quite irreconcilably
from both the plaintiff and his highly esteemed attorney, whom you
have heard saying that because of that murder Domaćinski is considered a hero, a meritorious man in the eyes of history, the nation,
future generations, and even of all eternity. . . ."

"It was a question of burglary by masked armed men, a deed
committed in self-defense, and as such it is not unlawful! It was
established at the time that the slandered man had not exceeded the
limitations of his defense! All that you have been telling us is nonsense! Do you understand? Nonsense!" yelled Domaćinski's lawyer
at the top of his lungs.

"Not even on this question of 'nonsense' do I agree with you,

Dr. Hugo-Hugo. *Defensio debet esse proportionata.* How could he
have otherwise killed the third man near the arbor and the fourth at
the other end of the vineyard near the fence, when that peasant
tried to jump over it in a hopeless effort to escape? If it were in crucial self-defense, why did the peasant start running away without
firing a single shot? I wanted to check the minutes on the case but,
of course, they are not there, they have disappeared. . . . But one
thing is unquestionable: the third and fourth peasants were shot in
the vineyard while trying to escape, and the first two at the entrance
to the cellar. Masked and armed burglars do not usually go to a
cellar to fetch a liter of wine. Moreover, I discovered in a quite insignificant domestic news report of those days carried by a local
daily that, according to the findings of the commission, the four
men were shot in the back. So, if I were to make any logical decision on this question, I would not in the least agree with the preceding speaker that Mr. Domaćinski deserved a memorial on account
of his famous deed, and even *aere perennius,* a memorial to show
posterity that he was a hero and a champion of justice and ethics.
This whole case should be considered in the light of paragraph two
hundred ninety-eight of the Penal Code, which unambiguously and
clearly states: if a person provokes another man by indecent conduct or a criminal act directly intended to injure him, the one who
insults may be acquitted. But this is not the question in this particular case. The question is of that gentleman boasting to us all of
having 'shot four men like four mad dogs,' and of his also threatening to kill me 'as the fifth mad dog.'

"I was provoked by the morally sick retelling of a criminal deed
that undoubtedly consisted of a quadruple murder; and what has
been described as a slander in the indictment, that is, that I alleged
that Domaćinski wanted to shoot me like a dog and reached for a re-

volver actually to shoot me is the truth, and therefore no slander at all. He reached for his revolver in reality. . . ."

"That is not true! Prove it!"

"What am I to prove? Everybody who was present on that veranda could see the revolver. . . ."

"That is not true! Nobody saw the revolver! It was a silver cigarette case. . . . You were drunk and to you the silver cigarette case seemed like a revolver. . . ."

Laughter in court. I admit that in that place, at that moment, it made me very nervous.

"Regardless of this simian laughter behind my back, I declare and I am ready to affirm up to my last days that Domaćinski did not hold in his hand a cigarette case, but a revolver."

"Watch out," two or three voices were heard from the public. Evidently this was a sign of dissatisfaction with my remark about simian laughter.

"Don't argue with the public! It is not your business! Stick to the subject," Dr. Attila von Rugvay warned me, and his obviously partial reprimand only intensified my unrest.

"Your duty is to tame those monkeys behind my back! That highly cultured elite does not see anything funny in the fact that a person has shot four men, but they are laughing because that person did not kill the fifth too."

"I forbid you to use that tone any more! Do you understand me? It is for the court to decide whether something is or is not in order. Stick to the subject!"

"The subject is concerned with insult and the notion of insult. The law prescribes that the notion of insult should be determined by sensible court practice. Who among us in this courtroom represents sensible court practice? Dr. Hugo-Hugo interprets a quadruple murder as a heroic deed, an act worthy of respect, a meritorious deed in the eyes of the people and the homeland. These gentlemen behind my back find it ridiculous if a person considers a revolver to be a revolver and not a cigarette case. Dr. Attila von Rugvay, who sits here in the name of Justice, a blind goddess, and who has in this incident not missed a single opportunity for displaying his partiality to my detriment . . ."

"Would you put these words of the defendant in the minutes," Dr. Attila von Rugvay turned to the court clerk, pointing with his finger to the minutes. "Dr. von Rugvay, who was seated here in the name of Justice, did not up to this incident miss a single opportunity to prove how partial he was to my detriment . . .' "

"To my detriment," the court clerk repeated after Dr. von Rugvay like an echo, and his tongue appeared between his two gaping front teeth so that he looked like a feeble-minded child writing dictation at a school desk, repeating it word by word after the teacher.

" 'To my detriment,' period. Are you finished?"

" 'To my detriment,' period."

"Okay, now write: 'Since the defendant has from the beginning of the trial disturbed the order of the court proceedings by his improper behavior, after having been warned against this at least five times and after having insulted the Court by his statement, he is sentenced to ten days' imprisonment according to paragraph two hundred thirty of the Penal Code."

" 'To ten days' imprisonment under paragraph two hundred thirty of the Penal Code.' "

"Good. Period. 'The accused is warned that, according to paragraph two hundred thirty-three of the Penal Code, he may not appeal against this decision, and if the defendant continues his provocative behavior, the Court will be compelled to remove him. . . .' Have you got that?"

"Yes, I have."

"The only thing," I interjected, "is that you did not quote me word for word. What I said was: 'Dr. Attila von Rugvay, who was seated here in the name of Justice, *a blind goddess.*' "

In the righthand corner of the courtroom, on a huge cupboard, like a cripple missing one arm, a sword in the other, was a plaster cast of Justice, probably a copy of one from above the doors of a big public building. That blind goddess in her richly pleated peplum, holding in her hand a vertical, sharp-bladed Roman sword (there were no scales, since her right hand with the scales was missing), that sad figure on the cupboard, dusty, dirty, forgotten, placed *ad acta* on a filing cabinet, appeared to me at that moment to embody the full meaning of these unavoidable court proceedings in the really fatal sense; *ad acta.* The verdicts are pronounced in this room today according to the laws of this torso, who is absolutely silent, deaf and dumb in the twilight on that antiquated cupboard and, in the name of Justice, Dr. Hugo-Hugo, for instance, asks me to bow to and obey the eventual sentence, although behind that torso is absolutely nothing; two or three tin chamber pots with the trademark of the factory 'Domaćinski Ltd.' engraved on them, two or three dead bodies in the vineyard near the arbor, and this Justice on the cupboard has no right hand and so it cannot weigh the case to find out what is in fact the insult, what the reply, which the revolver and which the cigarette case. . . .

In a lyrical mood, a little tired, at an enormous distance from everything that was part of my immediate reality, once again challenged by Dr. Attila von Rugvay "to speak if I had anything to say," I was absorbed in thought that was, it seemed to me, unquestionably sublime. But, judging from the reaction to my lyrical meditations among some of those present, it dawned on me that my personal impression of having spoken calmly and more or less absent-mindedly was not entirely in accordance with the fact. I said approximately that Domaćinski would have behaved in the most manly and chivalrous way if he himself, on his own initiative, had appeared in court because of that quadruple murder, since its verdict would maintain one of the fundamental principles of society: the principle of Justice. . . .

"To prove to Dr. Hugo-Hugo or his client that this is so would suggest that they should play a role for which that type of man has never displayed the least talent—the role of a man with balanced taste. I am fully aware of the futility of my effort to explain to those wise gentlemen that in life there are performances in which it is far better for the actor in the title role to fail than for the whole theater to perish."

"He's an old intriguer!" Dr. Hugo-Hugo began shouting nervously, turning his face toward the auditorium and pointing at me with both hands as I stood before the judge. "He is slyly diverting your attention from the principal matter to secondary ones, Honorable Court. What the defendant has been saying is sheer nonsense. Who is the leading actor here; who is playing the title role; who is the person who has provoked this whole affair? Domaćinski or him? It's all demagoguery. That is how one appeals to the lowest instincts. It is all nonsense. . . . If anybody is doomed to failure in this performance, it is certainly going to be you, Doctor. This performance of yours, in which you have taken the role of a righteous man, is very poor acting. No fairground hullabaloo or invocation of so-called social ghosts is going to save you. . . . We know this kind of trick too well."

"Doctor, would you allow the defendant to finish what he has to say, providing he sticks to the subject," Attila von Rugvay interrupted Dr. Hugo-Hugo in order to convince the audience of his impartiality.

"All right, but he has insulted the Court and the trial, Justice and me personally—as well as my client—and I am not here to listen passively to irresponsible offense from a hysterical man. Let the gentleman control himself or I shall be compelled to extend the indictment by adding new offenses and slanders. . . ."

"Everything will be entered in the record, Doctor. It is up to you to speak now. It's your turn."

It was again my turn to speak. I looked at my watch and, seeing the minute hand as it moved on quickly from one second to another, in a perfectly closed circle—which is absolutely nonsensical, by the way—I remembered the hourglass I used to see on the obituary page: two triangles, and the sand falling from one triangle to the other. In general, everything is like the sand in hourglasses; everything. The words, the courts, the evidence, the passions, the courtrooms . . . Everything—just sand. . . . The hand indicated three minutes to two exactly. The sky outside was suddenly covered with clouds, the window panes in the courtroom were clattering in the February snowstorm. At the other end of the courtroom they had lighted the gas, and this light intensified the melancholy aspect of the grim performance, which reminded me of a funeral procession. All faces were pale, exhausted; everything was tedious and boring. It was already getting late. It had to end.

My concluding remarks smoldered within me and then exploded like a mine in a stone quarry. It was like what happens when you shoot off fireworks and everybody believes that the last rocket has been exploded when the crowning burst appears and the whole area is suddenly illuminated by a supernatural light.

"Domaćinski," I said, "in the words of his lawyer, has become a demi-god who wished to survive in his half-educated and imaginary greatness for the whole of posterity and to be more lasting than bronze itself. This is how this magnificent hymn came about. It may command the admiration of future generations, but not mine, by any means. Never has a motif from a lawyer's speech been transformed more dishonestly than by this absolutely prosaic, banal, commonplace image of Domaćinski posing as a patrician, a wise and righteous man, constructor and benefactor in one. Everything that has ever been invented in human literature to honor or magnify heroes and great fighters has been reduced by my esteemed comrade Dr. Hugo-Hugo to phrases not only unconvincing but simply provocatively untrue. Domaćinski has been described to us as the personification of heroism, ethics, justice, goodness, and as a guide to future generations. When we take cognizance of everything that took place at that dinner party in the vineyard—when Domaćinski threatened to shoot me like a dog, since I criticized his famous quadruple murder, and when, unquestionably, he reached for his revolver to shoot me—we should logically put the question: do we all lack the shame required to safeguard the daily equilibrium of our own dignity, which is felt even in the lowest stratum of people? No promiscuous woman, for instance, would dare climb to the pulpit in church and preach about moral piety. Any of our assassins would have been ashamed had all the bells in our churches rung in their honor. And just the contrary is true before the Court, where the lies, flattery, and deceitful tricks of paid lawyers have indeed succeeded in disturbing every decency. Had this not been the case, applause would not have been heard in this court at times when the lies were most conspicuous. I do not believe, I do not want to and cannot believe such concoctions, because I am not a paid orator, flatterer, beneficiary, and whatnot of Mr. Domaćinski, and I do not think that he should be allowed to praise murder only because he exports his chamber pots to Persia."

"He is right! Congratulations! May you live long, blessed be your mother, well done, God bless you, may you live long, bravo!" someone shouted at the top of his voice at the other end of the court-room as if a fire had broken out. . . . The ladies Aquacurti-Sarvaš-Daljski and Maksimirski were disturbed, and Dr. Attila von Rug-vay hysterically yelled at the unknown noisemaker: "Who is it?"

"It's me, Mr. Chairman, if you please! That man was right. I served Domaćinski. He is a cad. There is not another like him in the whole world."

"And who is it that's shouting?"

"Haven't I told you it's me, Mr. Chairman? My name is Petar Krneta. I know Domaćinski. That man is right: he is a cad and should be put in jail."

"Out! Throw him out!"

Everybody jostled in an effort to throw out Petar Krneta. The members of the elite behind my back moved in their sheepfolds and began bleating as if the wind had brought the smell of a wolf into this nasty-smelling warm room. These silver foxes, the costly bracelets, the educated and musical, well-brought-up elite began to make noises, to move about, disturbed by the shouts, the banging of chairs, doors, and thundering footsteps on the wooden floor. One could hear Petar Krneta shouting outside in the corridor, "Bless the one inside, bless his mother, he is a decent man, leave me alone, I am not guilty of anything, long live the speaker, my congratulations to him!"

"Just see for yourself, Doctor, the fruits of your irresponsible con-duct." Dr. Hugo-Hugo turned to me, obviously upset and showing signs of sincere social revulsion. "Here you are, you may feel proud. It is either a commonplace naive demagoguery or paranoia."

"And when you alleged with reference to Domaćinski that the foreign authorities of the time had thrown him out of the civil service because of his political convictions, is that not paranoia?"

"What paranoia? These are facts."

"So those are facts? Please, go and find your facts in the municipality of Upper Miholj, and then you will have the honor to find out that your highly esteemed model patriot 'who had been thrown out of the civil service by the then foreign administration' was not sacked by the foreign administration because of his boldly declared political convictions, but for being a common embezzler. In his capacity of municipal executor in the municipality of Upper Miholj, he embezzled a considerable sum of money and was dismissed after an investigation and not because of boldly advocating his political convictions in opposition to the foreign rule. You see, Doctor, these are facts, and as for your dithyramb, it is sheer paranoia."

For the first time since the beginning of the performance, the public was obviously impressed, excited by my statements. Silence.

Hugo-Hugo, an experienced hand, rose to his feet calmly and without a single gesture of protest asked the esteemed court to enter into the record my latest statement. He added that he would extend his indictment, according to paragraph 301, because of the latest slander.

Dr. Attila von Rugvay asked me with an unconcealed smile of irony whether I still had something to say.

"I have."

"Go ahead."

"We have heard the Doctor say as Domaćinski's lawyer that that spirit that is 'as energetic as the whirlwind,' that that 'giant creator of the monumental foundations of our well-being,' as an idealist, with rifle in hand, defended the national interests in 1918, at the time of national shipwreck. . . . In the days of national catastrophe, four years before then, in 1914, that same idealist defended the national interests by being a Sarajevo police informer. Then he sent people to the gallows."

"That is a perfidious lie," Dr. Hugo-Hugo remarked, evidently disturbed.

"It is, unfortunately, no perfidious lie, nor even paranoia, but an ordinary, trifling, almost insignificant truth."

"Please, will you enter this in the records? Again I want to extend the indictment according to paragraph three hundred one, because of this new slander: that my client sent people to the gallows, and so forth."

"For both cases, that is, the allegation about the embezzlement and being an informer, evidence will be given. Will you summon Minister Krobatin as a witness?"

"What has Minister Krobatin to do with this? What are these new tricks?"

"Minister Krobatin came to see me two days ago on his own initiative and gave me some documents that show that in 1914 Domaćinski, a traveling salesman at the time for a monks' cheese factory in Bosnia, was a Sarajevo police informer and because of that many people were arrested. To me it all seemed unimportant, as I did not intend to defend myself at all. But after I found myself being treated by the Court as a case of paranoia and an irresponsible slanderer, I had to refer to Minister Krobatin and his documents. Moreover, I insist that all those persons present at the dinner party in the vineyard should be interrogated as witnesses, to establish how Domaćinski reached for his revolver to shoot me like a dog."

"These are all the most ordinary, the most prosaic provincial lawyers' tricks," Dr. Hugo-Hugo yelled excitedly, making nervous gestures in front of the green desk of the high forum. "This is escaping responsibility, a hysterical fear of the just Court."

"I am referring to the evidence, I am inviting witnesses, so it is only logical that I should insist that the trial be put off. And for the next trial, I request that Dr. von Rugvay not be the judge."

"Please enter the Doctor's statement: 'I request that another judge be appointed . . .' "

"Please," I said, "put down: 'because he does not believe in the judge's impartiality. First, because of mutual personal dislike, or even more than that: hatred. Second, because Dr. von Rugvay wanted to marry my daughter and I rejected him. He asked for a three-storied house as dowry, and I refused to give it to him. Not because of the three-storied house, but because I did not want to have such a man as a son-in-law. I would have given him the three-storied house and even the daughter, possibly, had she wanted him, but I do not trust him by any means.' There is another objection that disqualifies Mr. Rugvay to be judge in this case of quadruple murder and one attempt on life. But this objection need not be entered into the minutes. It is of a private nature."

"Please, Doctor, just carry on with your dictation. . . ."

"Then, put down: 'Arpad Rugvay, Attila's father, shot twenty-seven voters at Banska Jaruga. . . . Arpad's career was based on that mass massacre and Attila, logically, reacts too neurotically, or rather sentimentally, to even the faintest allusion to murder as a moral problem. . . . Brought up in a family where personal happiness, career, almost the whole growth of the family stemmed from a mass massacre . . .' "

"It is all paranoia, gentlemen, it is just paranoia!" thundered Dr. Hugo-Hugo's voice in the noisy courtroom.

The trial was adjourned.

7

BEHIND BARS

I was sentenced to eight months' imprisonment for insults and slanders, and the second performance in court was far less attractive than the first from the technical or, should I say, scenographic point of view. Instead of Attila, a decent and polite man was seated at the green desk, and Dr. Aurel Hermansky replaced Hugo-Hugo as Domaćinski's lawyer. He, too, was decent and polite. The whole trial passed without special incident. Answering the questions put to me only with "Yes" or "No," I was absolutely passive. Hermansky conducted the proceedings exclusively as a lawyer. The witnesses were in the main confused as well as insincere and, as for the material truth, their statements, as usual, differed. Some declared that Domaćinski had not reached for the revolver and that I was the first to do so; others stated they could not remember anything: wine, nerves, the particular circumstances, social considerations, love of truth, dignity, reputation, sympathies and antipathies, and the like. Most of the witnesses thought that the cigarette case glittering in my hand was a revolver and that the revolver in Domaćinski's hand was indeed a cigarette case. Mistaken assumptions on both sides. My chief witness—the "star" witness, as one might say—Minister Krobatin, did not appear in court. He excused himself because of bronchitis, on the strength of a medical certificate. On his behalf, Dr. Hermansky, Domaćinski's lawyer, read Krobatin's statement in which he confirmed my statements in principle: that he really had the document showing Domaćinski was in the secret service of the Sarajevo police in 1914, that he had really offered the document to me to use at my trial, but that I had refused to do this, saying "I was absolutely uninterested in the whole affair." Minister Krobatin especially emphasized that I was right, in his opinion, to believe on the basis of that authentic document "that Domaćinski had actually been in the secret service of the Sarajevo police," but at the moment, unfortunately, he was no longer in a position to make public this piece of evidence, since he had returned it to the confidential files. If it appeared necessary during the trial, he might name the official who had at the time made a copy of the document. As for Krobatin's information that he had given me confidentially, i.e., that Domaćinski had been dismissed from the civil service and charged with embezzlement, Minister Krobatin had been misled by irresponsible rumors not founded on fact. Domaćinski was, in fact, dismissed from the civil service, but that had been more than forty years ago, and the cause was not embezzlement, but irregularities in the treasury.

As the balance was returned to the treasury in good time—it was really a trifling sum, the matter was settled, as it is said, to everyone's mutual satisfaction.

All in all, the trial proceeded without a hitch, calmly, decently, according to the civil law. I expressed my satisfaction with the verdict, as did Domaćinski's lawyer Dr. Aurel Hermansky, and thus the unpleasant affair was ended and taken off the agenda. According to the rules of that same civil law, I was moved to a room with a straw mattress full of bedbugs; I have been lying on it since April. I lie on my back, my arms folded under my head, staring at the bright green moonlight, contemplating the deep and mysterious meaning of everything that has happened to me in my life, reliving time and again my disastrous breach with Vanda. Had I not lost Vanda, I might have lived a normal life, following my basic instincts. In that case I would not have been affected by a whole series of contradictions. My life would not have been illusory.

Vanda was married to a subaltern Hungarian district official at Munkacs. I met her twenty-three years ago, at the Stanislavov railway station, in the fall of 1915, when she was on her way back from Lvov, where she had been to visit her wounded husband, an officer in a Hungarian infantry regiment. She was my elder by three or four years, and our obscure, poisoned love, that of mature people hungry for affection, became a wild, tempestuous, blind passion. On the enervating and upsetting journey between Stryj, Munkacs, and Stanislavov Vanda reached a decision: she arrived one day in Budapest to join me, informing her husband that she had made up her mind to go away with me. We took a room in a hotel in Budapest, sometime in early fall in 1916. One could hear the crickets from the meadows in Budapest; on the other side of the Danube, like the last honors to a doomed love affair, a silent garland of gaslights glittered. I remember a Persian rug stretched over an otto-

man in the hotel room. It was roughly woven, and it was hurting
my knees. The room was dark, the blinds were pulled down. I
could not see anything except a vague mass of white female flesh in
a black silk petticoat. There was an intoxicating smell of Vanda's
cypress powder. And then there was a knock on the door.

"Who's there?"

"A telegram for the lady."

The telegram was from her husband. It had been despatched
from Munkacs and announced that that morning at eleven o'clock
their seven-year-old daughter had died of tonsillitis, and he begged
of her a last service: that she should come back for the girl's funeral.

Vanda left for the funeral of her seven-year-old little girl right
away, taking the first train. I knew she had left for good and that
she would never come back. When the red light at the back of her
train could no longer be seen from the Budapest railway station, I
was left alone on the platform, unable to understand anything.

Vanda's child was dead, Vanda had left for the funeral, Vanda
would not come back any more. . . . As if half asleep, I took a cab
in front of the station; I do not remember now how I reached the
park where the zoo was. There was an amusement program in the
park for soldiers, and it was the driver's idea to leave me there.
From time to time rockets were fired, and in their red reflection I
could see pink flamingos in their cage, standing on one leg and doz-
ing while I sipped wine like thick and clotted blood. On the verge
of despair, in that zoo near the concrete flamingo cage, I drank myself to a stupor so as not to commit suicide, not to scream at the
top of my voice, not to run into that mob of war benefactors and
soigné gentry, not to reach for my revolver.

Where is that woman now? Silent, flexible, obedient, compas-

sionate, with black circles under her eyes; the mother who believed
in utter foolishness that she was personally responsible for the death
of her child, because the little girl had really complained of a pain
in her throat the night before she left; but preoccupied by her own
problems, she had paid no special attention to the child's complaint.
... Vanda trembled at even the most delicate touch, she melted like
wax in her feverish delirium, her voice was soft, a little vague, and
her eyes, green as water in May, bottomless, wide, like the distance
in the spring. . . . The drums, the engines, the stations, that foolish
last night in the Budapest zoo: a lion awakened by the glitter and
explosion of the rockets, dragging his tufted tail along the floor of
his cage. . . . The bloody belly of the lion dragged around the cage,
his sulphurous eyes glittering.

Where are the wonderful nights we spent together on the river,
the nights in a boat that glided silently on the black surface, softly
touching the enormous flat leaves of the white water lilies; in the
dewy forest under the ruins of an ancient city in the Carpathians,
among the owls, in a thunderstorm, in the cellar of an old neglected
fort? Where are our illusions that flourished in empty churches, in
train compartments, in pastry shops from Stanislavov to Munkacs?
Everything has disappeared under the waves of shelling, buried under the piles of new events that have taken away our miserable de-
ception like a tiny paper boat carried by the water. . . .

The first snow has come, my boots are torn, and the water inun-
dates my toes and sticks to them. I am in my trench, my rags are
completely wet and muddy, the snow in the loopholes is also wet;
my coat is soaking wet, heavy and wrinkled; my face is unshaven;
I look like a prisoner; my face shows acute pain. I am staring at the
mud, the fog, the snow, I am waiting for a shell—it will be a salu-
tory one, no doubt—in the head, in the heart, in the intestines. . . .

I am waiting for pneumonia or typhus. . . . But nothing happens, and nothing happened, nothing essentially changed between then and now.

There are individuals who cannot adapt themselves to circumstances. The great majority do bookkeeping (double-entry, too, mind you); the vast majority settle things according to the rules and regulations; the great majority do not seek any imaginary or nonexistent way out; the majority pleasantly, beautifully, and humbly obey the higher factors both in this world and the world to come; the great majority work—obeying and working, they are not in fear of their own vacuums. The great majority are doing fine. They are all right. The great majority play bridge, snore, smoke, sniffle, and, trumpeting through their bodily cavities, do very well in the universe; to all appearances, this is the only way of doing well in the universe: you break wind as if you were playing a pipe and simultaneously fill the space around you with your social prestige. Someone else snores, and it is the only way of settling the enigma of the universe. Therefore you should snore and be satisfied with the dignity of your snoring. I do not snore because I suffer from lack of sleep, and if I may be allowed to express myself figuratively, pathetically, almost in an old-fashioned way: I sit and gnaw my nails in solitude. I am wide awake, I do not sleep, I have been transformed into the most vigilant of night watchmen over my own conscience. In fear and in boredom I listen to the clock striking the hours at night, and my vigils either have or do not have any special meaning.

If man could reconcile his own contradictions, if he could overcome the extremely intricate situations around him, he would settle the disorder within and around him, he would add meaning to the universal nonsense around and within him according to a special

self-defense system he has, which is called, in everyday vulgar par-
lance, "an outlook on life."

Since we are stuck in this confused, chaotic, and unsettled
world and have our own outlooks on life, it is easier to sail with
a compass, however cheap it may be, than according to the stars,
especially when it is cloudy, as it is in our case. Burglar Matko,
the owner of the tortoise Geraldine in No. 47, has his iron, revolver-
like "outlook on life." He has been in jail serving various sentences
for about seventeen years, and now he is being investigated, charged
with a naive little theft and, as soon as he is free again, "he will
either escape abroad as a rich man or end up on the gallows."
Burglar Matko, Domaćinski, my wife Agnes, her baritone, everyone has his or her own "outlook on life." I, unfortunately, do not
have one; and what is even more disastrous for my intellectual and
moral standard: I have never had one. If one could solve the question of one's own mysterious fate by means of an "outlook on life,"
with a revolver or sleeping pills, or by means of any other toy,
whether it be a woman, cards, horses, a career; if one could clarify
one's ideas by an ideological purgative; if there were a shop or a
store dealing in "outlooks on life," you could enter such a shop,
bow to its owner, and buy several outlooks on life—the best, the
most comfortable, the most up-to-date. You could order several
dozens of each "outlook"; something to try and something to keep.
After making the necessary purchases, you would have enough
infernal phosphorus to illuminate your own darkness, and sleep
calmly, fully aware that no particular danger was lurking.

Well, Valent Polenta, a poor man from Stubice who often starved
on his two-and-a-half acres until at the age of forty-nine he became a relatively well-off vine-grower, now in pre-trial confine-

ment for shooting a forester who had caught him poaching, Valent Polenta, my cellmate who snores on the mattress next to mine, also has "an outlook on life" and is satisfied with it. His only concern is to extricate himself from his current situation in which he has to serve his six or seven years' imprisonment.

Having fought in the war for several years on various fronts, I have always admired the extraordinary, ingenious talent in our people for dealing with practical things, that precious ability to grasp the realities of life. For instance, the ability to shoe a horse without any equipment—neither fire, horseshoes, nor hammer. In a jiffy the fire is lighted, a piece of metal found, someone produces nails from his pocket, and the mare is shod. Or how, camping under the leaking roof of a dilapidated mortuary in a remote Galician cemetery with water up to one's knees, the whole region a sea of mud, tea is promptly made over a big fire built of crosses from the graves. Someone has found a dry haystack too; it is warm, the fire is burning, you can smell rum, and one fellow sleeps on a catafalque as if it were the most comfortable of beds. It takes talent to steal a goose, to fry pancakes, to use a sardine can to make a perfect lamp, to disappear without a trace when it comes to a lethal order from an unpleasant commander and to be unaffected by fear.

In all those insignificant manifestations of human resourcefulness I learned how to admire yet another precious quality of our people: that extremely refined instinct for assessing the inner moral merits of one's superior officer. It is a flair more keenly developed than a dog's sense of smell. Truly, intuition of a high degree. After the first words are spoken, our military people know with whom they have to deal: a cunning rascal or a good-natured man, a stupid but strict man, or a camouflaged skeptic who wears the mask of an officer but does not believe either in the orders he gives or the shallow phrases he shouts at the recruits whom he addresses.

All those qualities stemming from long experience in war and life were intensified in Valent Polenta.

A real expert in practical matters, Valent volunteered to light the stove, polish shoes, sweep the room, make tea, and empty the bucket. He kept all our possessions in perfect order—underwear, pillows, straw mattresses, and fur jackets. He cleaned the windows, sewed on buttons, served the food. He did the washing-up and the laundry, discovered where hot water could be found, how tobacco could be smuggled in; he was both my orderly and my mail carrier, my adviser and my companion; undoubtedly, one of the wisest, kindest, and most experienced persons I have ever met. He got accustomed to the mass of superfluities one drags around for the sake of one's comfort. Boxes and cases, nail scissors and eau-de-cologne bottles, soaps, razors, books, fountain pens, paper, letters, pocket knives, underwear, buttons, garters, tooth brushes, creams, combs, newspapers, magazines—in short, all the rubbish that illustrates the futility of our civilization was set out by Valent on the shelves and on the table with the tidiness of the perfect butler. He poured out warm water for me to wash; he wrapped all my books in newspaper; he caught pigeons on the window with a special gadget of willow wands that he himself both devised and mounted; he could play the accordion; he told me stories lasting whole nights (and in comparison with those stories our contemporary literature is nothing special); and when, at the beginning of the fall, I had influenza with a high temperature, Valent cured me with his own medicines—made tea for me, gave me orange juice, looked after me like his nearest and dearest; in brief, made a fuss over me because, as he admitted at our parting—clumsily, irrelevantly, rudely, unclearly, but sincerely—he himself liked me a little. Judging from everything he knew about me and heard from me in the eight months of our life together, Valent assured himself that among the people wearing overcoats there were human beings. The very realization that an individual may be a human being in spite of being a man of learning opened up to him a new outlook on life and the world, and inspired him with the hope that, after all, everything was not lost forever, that some solution would be discovered, and that all wisdom had not perished and all hearts were not dead.

Among my books, the *Manual of Buddhism* attracted Valent's utmost attention. The legend of a divine prince who had been conceived immaculately by a mother who was a queen, and a mysterious deity in the shape of a white elephant who had been formed in the womb of his sublime mother like a rainbow beam of celestial light and was born from her right armpit seven hundred years before Christ—that mysterious story from the Ganges fascinated Valent. Practically every day I had to read to him some of Buddha's teachings while he was mending underwear, sewing on buttons, polishing shoes, making tea or smoking. Later he would lie motionless and speechless for several hours, nodding his head and spitting while contemplating intricate ideas like nirvana, death, or the futility of earthly deceptions.

The gray autumnal twilight is closing in, and I am reading to my good companion Buddha's thoughts about the universe, about the stars, about suffering, about primeval matter, and about the man who wakes up in perfection when all thirst for life has been quenched within him, when he has rejected it completely, realizing that pleasure and satisfaction are the root of all evil.

On a gloomy November afternoon, rainy, boring, headachy, Valent Polenta expressed his own thoughts, revealing to me his outlook on life:

"A man is pulled out of his mother's womb like a bloody dog and, as soon as his teeth stop aching, his back starts hurting, and, unless he is hanged first, he dies like a decent person. He cannot escape his lot. Either he is going to be impaled or prick himself on a thorn; or a snake will bite him, or a gear will smash his thumb. And what comes next? He builds a house for himself, drags a young girl to bed; and what becomes of her? She turns into a matron who acts like a cherub but is a perfect devil. She prevents him from living a decent manly life; she taunts him constantly, sucks his blood, and when other people refer to him, they say, 'He is all right, he has a wife, God should give him peace of mind, he died like a decent man and left everything to his wife.' What can a man do with a wife? If a chicken perishes, she cries, but when I was brought home for the first time pierced by shots and bleeding like a stuck pig, what did she do? She began to curse me, calling me rascal and a thief, and predicting that I would end on the gallows. And when it became obvious that I might die after the forester had beaten me up, she sighed: 'God, what am I supposed to do'?

" 'What are you talking about, old woman? You'd better give me half a liter of wine to cure me. . . .'

"Do you think, Doctor, the old woman gave me wine?

" 'And if you drink up all the wine, what will be left for a cure if somebody else falls ill?' she asked.

"Then I got up, I stole everything the old woman had, demolished the house, and that is how I was cured.

"Was she beautiful? Better not ask! And what a cook! She made pies that not even the chickens wanted. She was a fine woman, as they say, but it would have been far better if I had lost her three times than met her once. She died of the Spanish flu soon after the war, and I ordered a beautiful oak cross for her—it cost me eleven florins. Above her open grave I said to myself: You will be an ass if you have anything to do with a devil again. And what do you think, Doctor? I dragged another wife to bed around carnival time. As the Chinese proverb says: A man is a tube with nine holes, and the ninth is both deaf and blind. . . .

"What man really has is a cellar and in it a lot of tasteless wine, and if he drinks it all, people say he is a drunken swine and a rascal. And how do men really live? They drive cattle to the fair because they cannot afford to eat the meat. They have to massage the hoofs of their cows, comb the oxen, empty the bowels of the mares and burn incense under their tails, and they themselves must die like beasts, and if this is not hell, what is the life of a peasant? The Chinese proverb is right. My dear Doctor, if you imagine that a young girl does not grow up into a stubborn, quarrelsome woman, you are mistaken again. And I will tell you, everything that is now happening to mankind is nothing but a huge funeral for an ass—everything is in a state of chaos. Once upon a time there was a king and he had a red sleeve. If you ask why he had a red sleeve, you are told to go to hell. Like clay on a potter's wheel, this is how we all turn— a vicious circle. I can assure you that this is so: whoever thinks about the earth and imagines it is his earth and that the universe is all ours—that man is lost because it is not so. My granny was quite right in saying that eventually all poultry and birds and everything living and crawling and moving about will be burned and die—the big bleeding dogs will rush in snarling, with bloody snouts, and everything will be submerged under a dunghill. The mindless will crush us and oppress and plunder us; whoremasters will yell that everything is in the best order as prescribed by law, and whoever does not agree is a rascal and should be hanged. Fire full of sulphur will burst from the hills, dead bodies will smell to high heaven, mad dogs and dead oxen will be on all sides.

"And this is how it has occurred, exactly as my granny predicted. This was what I remembered in the trench when bullets were whistling and bursting around me as I sat in the clay, and the half-dead soldiers—the death rattle. . . .

"When we were all mobilized in 1914, there was terrible confusion. We were torn to pieces on forked trees. We were chased and tormented the way a cat treats chickens in the yard. We were opened up, searched, and put together again. They butchered us so that there was not a single one of us who did not drag himself like Saint Roch, scabby and bleeding. But not even this was enough for them. They took away our boots and left us barefoot like pilgrims; they squeezed everything out of us; they made our bodies into sponges full of blood; they made mincemeat out of us. They pierced us all through with needles and scalpels. We lay on the operating table like children in bloody placentas. They sewed us up, patched us up and put us together again so that we could stand to attention in the unit, be slapped in the face, beaten with a rifle butt in the ribs and on the head, as if our heads were brought into this world to serve as targets on the rifle range. And what do we get from all this? A disabled war veteran's pension with which we can buy five boxes of matches. And not even that is paid any more.

"When we were mobilized, we were all alike: all the young men were slim, as if made of tin sheets—genuine dandies. New boots, new uniforms, new socks, new overcoats, new and freshly laundered underwear, and everything in the magazine was so well-polished and smelled so of naphthalene that we all squeaked and moved and swayed our hips like girls in front of a church. Like Lippizaners on parade, we rattled our military kits, cartridge boxes, bayonets, shovels, brimming breadsacks, rucksacks, and lamps that were tied to the kits to prevent them from moving during the march; and they also gave us a compass so that we would not get lost in the forest; we were given notebooks, too, to write down whatever we wanted to.

"My dear Doctor, it was funny even to look at us. Except for a silver watch, I looked as if I were dressed for confirmation.

"What else could happen? Everything was according to rule. A moratorium was enforced and your debts were annulled; your wife would get a war subsidy; you were given roast suckling pig and a piece of cake in a napkin; a five-crown piece was put in your pocket; you were given a red notebook and a long warm jacket, and bread as a reserve; you also got some tobacco; you were decorated with braid as if you were going to ask a girl to marry you and somebody had stuck a rose in your tunic. And there were also little things you got: a small paper bag, and some salt and paprika, if you wanted to add paprika to your canned food, and in another bag there were some bandages, if anything happened to you; if, God forbid, your head was hit, you could patch it up right away; and then there was a bottle of polish with a tiny cloth, and a brush for polishing buttons, and a special little brush for your greatcoat, so that you could brush it properly before you died, removing all the cornstalks and onion leaves, or you could brush your teeth after eating a good roast. . . .

"And this is what I think: if it came to a war again, I would not need all those things. I would cut a bit of bacon; I would shelter behind a willow tree, put two or three grenades into my pocket . . . and I would aim at one of those fellows responsible for our being here on our straw mattresses, lying like loaves of bread. This would be my own war strategy.

"And since we are talking about this strategy now called 'peaceful policy,' I must tell you that I have no idea about it. I do not understand it at all, my dear Doctor. Politics, if I may say, are rather like a mill, and I can only see that the political mill grinds us thoroughly, and even plays with us, and that it is all the same if something comes from the left or from the right; and if a person is caught in that trap, it seems to me, it is most unlikely he will be able to drag himself out of it.

"And I know some things for certain: what is too long should be cut short. If a hare is kicked, he is protected by his fur, but a man is naked, if you'll excuse me. A man is like a snail: anything can crush us. . . .

"When I was a little boy, in the winter I used to watch my grandmother, now dead, sitting at the loom and weaving, and I often thought that if her shuttle dropped, nobody could put it back. Everything seemed so strange to me, moving and turning in front of my eyes. And I could never understand how the various parts of the loom could fit and work together and that nothing went wrong, sliding up and down like a blackbird in a cage; everything seemed so clever, as if directed by a hidden guide. And once on All Saints' Day, when I had measles, I stayed at home, and when my grandmother went to church, I tried to weave like a man, a real weaver. But soon everything got tangled up, and my grandmother spanked me when she came back from church.

"Only a fool wants to sit at the loom and weave unless he is trained for the job and, really, weaving is not so complicated as politics. But every devil wants to meddle in politics and every fool dares to take the floor in its name. Our politics is like a weaver's workshop. Once inside, you get so enmeshed that there is no way out. . . ."

It was already late at night and I was still listening to Valent. The cathedral clock struck two. That rascal had been talking since four o'clock in the afternoon about otters, deer, birds, wars, women, politics; and every single word he said was rounded out by his knowledge of life and his innate talent.

The night hovers over the town; blind, foggy, a gray November night; and Valent discusses our problems, our misery, as logically and as convincingly as though his words were guidelines or proclamations and not clouds of hot air that evaporate in that little room that reeks of kerosene, wet straw mattresses, and the bucket washed out with carbolic acid.

Had Valent Polenta been educated, the things he was saying would perhaps not have meant much; but in his dry, sly, cunning but lofty humor, carried away by the wonderful serenity he enjoyed even in prison, he was an inexhaustible source of joy to me. Never in my life did I laugh so much as in the months I spent with him in prison, where I left him swallowing his tears. Today, when I think of him, I get a lump in my throat: I see him in rough prisoner's robes, hoeing around the potatoes in the vicinity of the Lepoglava penitentiary, completely unaware that I am longing for his company as one longs for the dearest comrade or friend.

8

TROUBLES
ON ALL SIDES

Once again a "free citizen" who is allowed to drink coffee and milk in whichever of the five cafés in our town suits him, I moved along the streets and frequented these public places—to the great amazement of my fellow citizens—as if nothing had happened. According to my own logic, nothing had actually occurred. But, logic or no logic, it was felt I had hurt a prominent citizen; I did not show sufficient respect for that prominent citizen, i.e., to the extent prescribed by law, and I was tangibly punished for that according to the same law: I served my eight-month sentence almost in penitence, virtuously spending the whole time in jail, and now, it seemed to me, the matter was finished.

However, just the opposite was true: the matter only now began to disturb the people in our town. In that filthy little backwater it was incomprehensible to the magpies that a bird among them could refuse to croak like a bird of prey over a carcass and could criticize violently the folly of society. All foolish people, just out of solidarity, began to generate psychological opposition to my conduct.

While being shaved at the barber's, I was thinking of the enormous number of my own ideas that I had forgotten. A brighter idea crosses the mind, or a whole series of intricate relations explains itself to the individual, and then suddenly the feeling of seeing things clearly fades and disappears.

"I beg your pardon, Doctor," said the barber, waking me from my thoughts (he waved his shining razor around my right eye). "I beg your pardon. Excuse me, but I would be interested to hear whether it is true that you are going to be put in jail again."

"In jail? Why?"

"I don't know, Doctor. Dr. Hermansky was here last night and he told us that he was extremely sorry; he likes you very much; and was convinced that you were well-meaning—but, well, this is how he put it—'an overstrained man with undermined nerves'; and that was why, although it was embarrassing for him, he would be compelled to raise accusations against you again on behalf of Director-General Domaćinski because, just as you did before the trial, you have been saying around town that Director-General Domaćinski is a bandit and a criminal type. . . ."

"Oh, forget those silly things. They are not in the least interesting."

"They are not, of course, Doctor, allow me to say."

"I won't allow anything. Do you understand me? I'll only allow you to soap my face and shave me. That's your business."

"I beg your pardon. I didn't mean to hurt you. But people are right. Don't you see how nervous you are? Why do you get so upset?"

If he had not been gesticulating around my neck with a razor, I would have slapped him. I am not nervous and I don't get upset, and he was poking his nose into my affairs and wanted to put me in jail because he shaved the Director-General's lawyer and because he is a stupid lackey.

My neighbors have been bothering me for years. They visit when it suits them; they suddenly turn up, annoy you like tedious flies circling around cowdung, they bother you again and again, talk nonsense, plaguing you for years about matters that have nothing to do with anybody. They talk about the interior decoration in my flat, this or that individual, someone's divorce, an exhibition or private competition for an assistant-professorship; and now even my own barber wants to bother me: am I again to be put in jail?; and why have I been saying that I am convinced Domaćinski is a criminal type, a bandit, and a born burglar?

For years I have been discussing with my neighbors things that do not interest me: diluvial fish; Cromwell; the English Constitution; the press; the wars. Whole years have been filled with empty talk; futile, boring, and repetitious. Now I must talk about Domaćinski fifteen hours a day with everybody, from the barber as he shaves me in the morning to the waiter in the Europe Café who, when I arrive there this evening, will serve my coffee with a little portion of cream along with the latest gossip: that Dr. Hugo-Hugo has hinted at a whole series of trials involving me, that Dr. von Rugvay declared to Director-General S. S. at the gambling house that he would not stop until I was beheaded.

On the way to the café I am stopped by Dr. B.R. who expresses his sympathy, regretting my having so deeply "gone astray into martyromanic psychosis."

"What you have been trying to achieve, my dear colleague, is worthy of a Saint Sebastian. You will be pierced by the spears and arrows of the law, so that in the end you will finish in the street like a beggar, like Lazarus, like Saint Sebastian."

The next man who came over to talk to me was Dizdar-Barjaktarević, the publisher of a vulgar magazine under the anarcho-individualistic and semi-symbolic title, *Atlantis. Atlantis,* according to Dizdar-Barjaktarević, symbolized Europe: a continent facing imminent catastrophe. Dizdar-Barjaktarević eventually developed into an ethnographic, folkloristic optimist. The only way out, he discovered, was folk embroidery, national tradition, popular ballads. He became a follower of Gandhi, wrote anti-Marxist polemics, dealt with anthroposophic matters, became a member of the directorate of semi-rightist youth groups preaching racism. He overnight became a contributor to his own paper and, under government auspices, was sent abroad. As I remember, it was rumored that he was a semi-official informer. Later he returned, published dubious almanacs, launched two or three weekly newspapers, again went abroad to very remote countries, came back again, and that is how finally he turned up at my café, sat down at my table, and from the first moment began to get on my nerves. I admit he irritated me in every way—his unpleasant bulldog appearance, his pimply face, his polished nails, his golden cigarette case (which he immediately described as worth 1,200 Swiss francs), his cheap soap, his feigned optimism, his toothless smile, his gestures, his voice, his intonation, the way he spoke; in brief: everything about him.

"Oh, good afternoon, Doctor. How are you? Why have you begun to play the part of a national tribune? I am so pleased to see you. And you've been in jail for a long time . . . that's no joke. . . . When people want to play the arbitrator, they must take the consequences. You know our proverb: Those who can't jump over the fence should not go to a dog's wedding. As for Domaćinski, I know him only too well. He is as clever as a fox. His name was on the list of the Sarajevo police. Of course it was. . . . But how can one prove it, my dear man? Yet I must admit one thing, Doctor. You are a stubborn man. Admittedly. But I have heard that Rugvay is starting a new offensive. . . . And other consequences, according to law will follow, unfortunately. And I am back from Athens. You know, I thought of Athens quite differently. I tell you, Doctor, nothing could be more provincial. And now I am on my way to Berlin. I am going to stay there a month or two. I don't really know why people grumble so much about the situation in our country. I have recently been all over Europe, and I can tell you frankly that there is not so much construction in any other country, not so many sites, not such creativity, not so much development. . . . From Berlin, I am going to Brussels—a tedious, unutterably Philistine city. . . ."

"Lucky man, you are always on the move—Paris to Athens, Athens to Berlin, Berlin to Brussels . . . and a whole year in Rome. You've been to Munich, to London, and even to Paris. I don't remember who told me you stayed for a long time in Paris. More than two years."

"Oh, yes. Paris, you say? I was in Paris for two or three years. I met Stravinsky. A fine man. A little conceited. Otherwise, a pleasant gentleman. But he has just one fault: my dear man, as a pianist, he bores his friends and he plays so badly that it is really sickening to listen to him. . . . Even Picasso invited me to come to see him in his house: he showed unusual interest in our frescoes. I promised Picasso I would write an introductory note for his exhibition in New

York. I had tea with Lhote. *Apropos* of Lhote, but just between ourselves: in the group around Lhote nobody appreciates our Meštrović. You know, Meštrović is a figure in our country. And what have we got? Njegoš, a few popular ballads, and Meštrović. I wanted to help him, I felt sorry for him, and I said to Lhote: You see, dear master, you cannot talk like that about our master. But he was stubborn and unyielding. They just wouldn't change their minds. They said: You can't compare him, for instance, to Bourdelle. What a distance he is from him. Of course, Bourdelle is not a trifle, but still . . . And that's how I got into trouble with Meštrović.

"You don't know I am a contributor to XX *Siècle*. Yes, yes, I wrote an article about architecture in the southern areas of our country. Really, they pay well: three thousand francs a quire. If the job weren't so boring, I might have become a writer. For instance, Plon. I spent the summer vacation with his wife and daughter at St. Tropez, and Plon implored me to write a book—some sort of monograph—about our country: he wanted to pay me two thousand Swiss francs a quire. Do you realize what that means? Yesterday, I heard it said—confidentially, of course, and this is also between ourselves—that Lantoš, you know that tramp, Lantoš—has written a monograph about what do you think? Guess. You'll never guess. Lantoš has written a monograph about Domaćinski. It's to be printed on glossy art paper in four-color typography. Dr. Hugo-Hugo has already paid him a good advance. Congratulations!

"*Apropos* of Domaćinski—this is between ourselves, but confidentially, Doctor—I know the man who gave Minister Krobatin a photostat of the documents kept by the Sarajevo police. You can have the authentic photostats. Now, don't misunderstand me. I am not acting as mediator, I am only warning you out of pure well-meaning friendship. . . ."

The notion of obtaining those documents was at first juridically attractive. But that pimply snout in front of me, that Dinaric type, was physiologically repulsive to me.

"Thank you. I am not interested in the matter at all. It is all over as far as I am concerned."

"Doctor, it is a question of a trifling sum of money: the man wants five thousand. . . . For you it is a question of great importance. You have embarked on a struggle with crocodiles. Be careful."

"Thank you."

"You really don't want them?"

"No, thank you."

"Is that your last word?"

"Well, my dear fellow, do you understand the meaning of the phrase 'No, thank you?' No, thank you."

"Oh? Resignation? You see, Doctor. Fits of silent melancholic resignation are always reliable signs of a lost battle. This means that wisdom has prevailed. One is reconciled to facts. Well, Domaćinski does not rank among people overwhelmed by melancholy. Domaćinski has hired Lantoš, and Krobatin's man, who, between ourselves, is a thief and dangerous scum, has a whole collection of documents . . . I don't know whether it is authentic but Domaćinski is offering me fifty thousand if I hand him over the document. . . ."

"What document?" I asked. "Who would deliver the document? To whom?"

"Why are you playing the fool? The document, my dear man, the police document, showing clearly that you denounced Dr. Werner under your own signature in 1914. . . ."

At that moment I slapped the blackmailing liar who, in 1914, the year I was snoring in jail on account of my anti-imperial convictions, was decorated by the Austrian Emperor for bravery, honor, and glory on the battlefield. That fatal loud slap came about according to all the rules of wisdom and logic. A big commotion. The waiters. Much noise. A small apprentice waiter who happened to be passing by at the moment, carried away by what was happening, spilled five or six glasses of beer on the ladies at the next table. The clinking of the broken glass against the marble floor, the ladies shrieking, the guests, the astonished guests in the café, the waltz from *La Traviata,* the police, the interrogation behind the bar, the jostling of a whole pack of old ladies around us; in brief—a scandal at the Café Central. . . . The result: a five-day imprisonment at the police station without the possibility of converting the sentence into a fine because after the "Von Petretich case" it was the second "case" of inciting a disturbance in a public place. And a few days later, soon after I returned from jail, there was the third case of inciting a disturbance in a public place—this time at the Café Europe.

I was seated, reading a newspaper at the café—an article by an expert about poison gas attacks on European cities and about the socially selective advantages of such attacks. The author of the article correctly assumed that it was chiefly the overpopulated sections of a large city that would be victimized in the event of a well-planned attack with poison gas—that is, the sections inhabited by the demoralized city dregs. Since today, with our high degree of technology and mechanized production, unskilled manpower is, in the main, absolutely superfluous, a poison-gas attack on a large industrial city would, among other things, have the virtue of getting rid of our human trash.
"Hello!"
"Hello!"
"May I?"
"Please do."

"How are you?"

"Okay, thanks. And you?"

"Me, too. Thank you."

It was my schoolfellow Franjo Ljubičić, who from childhood was nicknamed Francek. He was a bank clerk who had been thrown out of the bank and was at present in charge of accounting with a customs agent, and was looking for a better job. He told me he needed the aegis of a prominent director of a reputed bank, how everybody was involved in embezzlement and cheating, how everything was based on theft and fraud, and how the people were malicious and corrupt. And how were things with me? He had heard from someone that action had been taken to revoke my doctor's diploma because I did not deserve the title. He had heard that Domaćinski had paid me well and that I had made good money....

"How do you mean, Domaćinski? Why should Domaćinski have paid me?"

"Now listen, for God's sake, please don't pretend. If someone has evidence of the truth and can use it, and does not make use of it but acknowledges his sentence, and even without an appeal, well, by God, things are not done like that for no reason. Between old friends—*entre nous*—how much did you get?"

"And even you believe I took a bribe from Domaćinski and that this explains why I did not take the case to a higher court?"

"And why shouldn't I believe it? Nobody has ever heard of a case where a person had the proof in his hand and still acknowledged the sentence and went to jail for eight months. A funny business. Who would not have accepted? In the whole world there is no individual who cannot be bribed. Don't be angry, for God's sake, I don't blame you in the least. But just between old friends—"

"Excuse me, but if you believe I could take money from Domaćinski, I think our conversation is absolutely superfluous. Only the

fact that we are in this overcrowded café prevents me from reacting
to your words as would be logical: by slapping you in the face. . . .
Please leave my table at once and leave me alone."

"You want to send me away from this table? This table belongs
to me as much as to you. Get out of here, you old swine. Cad!"

The two or three last phrases "old swine—get out of here—cad"
—were howled by Francek Ljubičić so loudly that everybody
around us raised his head in alarm, wondering what would happen
to me now, an old and tried provoker of scandals in public places.
I remember the situation clearly. I felt really awkward, blushing
and squirming like a worm. And yet, you must forgive me, for, de-
spite the respect one can feel for politeness, it is an unpleasant experience to be the object of a hue and cry, disturbed by prying looks
and meeting impertinence on all sides. . . . Still holding in my hand
the café's copy of the newspaper I turned over all the glasses and
cups on the table, and all the silver in front of Francek, thus symbolically explaining to both of us that everything was over between
us. Let him go.

Wet with coffee, water, and tea from the silver teapot that had
spilled directly into his lap, Franjo Ljubičić rose to his feet, and in
a routine fashion, like a boxer, he punched me in the eye. I regained
consciousness in the clinic, where I lay for two weeks absolutely at a
loss about the fate of my left eye, since the blow had fallen with its
full weight on the cornea, and so the risk of blindness was indeed
considerable. For a full thirty days I was in a completely dark room
with drawn black curtains, and those thirty days were the last thirty
quiet and harmonious days in that part of my disturbed and upset
life.

I was lying in a room darkened by black curtains. What is a
lonely man among those immense passions and blind prejudices?

What can a man do in a shipwreck without a lifebelt? Our days
pass with our lives like Twentieth-Century Fox newsreels. The news
appears on the screen of reality at an ever more maddening speed;
the play of light and shade, the mysterious performance of European lies grows increasingly obscure and enigmatic every day, the
public's horror is increasingly intensified, and nobody can tell when
the bombs dropped on Madrid or Shanghai that we watch from our
seats in the cinema will be dropped on our own heads. Just as in
popular theaters in China, we sleep in the auditorium, we eat there,
we live there, and we die there. Being present at a magic performance, acting as both actors and spectators, without being able to
tell one from the other, we do not make out who is watching whom:
whether it is the actors who watch the public or the other way
around. We watch but we, too, are equally watched. The newspapers, the troubles, the noisy processions of people, the moths
banging inside the lighted gas lamp on the veranda—a man who
has been asleep for more than thirty years has awakened, and, under
the strong influence of an insignificant, perfectly logical, extremely
clear, and quite understandable truth, directed himself toward confusion. People generally do not like discussions about the truth being not what we are prone to believe. For, after all, what is truth?
My own life's truth, what is it? The rivers flow, the rain falls, beams
from soldiers' barracks quiver at night in the fog. For a short while
I had been calm and composed with Jadviga Jesenska in an ordinary
dirty hotel room.

   I was lying in my room with black curtains and could not understand the most essential question. Was it a question of the beginning of a cure, or was I eventually to go blind and thus remain in
a dark room, in my own solitude, absolutely alone? Or was I only
now facing battles, whereas everything so far had been a quiet,
idyllic overture before the crash in which I was probably going to

lose my head because I would not surrender or betray the banner? Had I a banner at all? Were not perhaps the dark shadows around me in this room the flickering of a dying oil lamp? The long shadows quiver before they are extinguished forever, and this around me is only a silent forecast of the final, pleasant, and last darkness.

What does it mean when life is reduced to bestialized pictures of murder? Life has always been purest and deepest where it is announced in a mysterious moment of beauty: the widespread dark gray wing of a pigeon with blue glittering silvery nuances of the warm spring sky; a young poplar quivering against the sky in the early morning hours. . . . I must go, I must go from this frightful room darkened with black curtains to a light blue daybreak somewhere far in the south. . . . The door of the quiet lonely little house at the end of a row of trees squeaked; a white kid peeped out from between two stone pillars; the morning breeze blew above a span of wavering dewy lawn; the birds twittered above the laurel and oleander groves. . . . Frascatti, Grottaferrata, Castel Gandolfo, like the melody of a light blue symphony, a transparent pianissimo of the outlines of the Albanian mountains . . . the pine trees, the cypresses, the murmuring of the water in the fountains . . . the light brown of a heavy, dark, gold-framed Renaissance painting. A well murmured in the shadow of an oak, the white clouds flew above the province, the cowbell rang, and one could hear a flute. An idyll.

9

INTERMEZZO IN
THE SISTINE CHAPEL

I did not lose my eye. I left the clinic and was sent to prison for eighteen days "for inciting disorder in a public place"; then I went to Italy: roaming and traveling through Umbria—Perugia, and Siena in the Spring, Rome at Easter. My Italian tour, and especially the sojourn in Rome and everything that happened in the Sistine Chapel, took on the contour of another scandal back home: it was rumored that in the Sistine Chapel I had had a fit of ungovernable fury: I had jumped on the main altar and from the main altar, below Michelangelo's "Last Judgment," I snatched an enormous silver candelabrum and injured an old English woman; as was only natural, I had then been put in a strait jacket and incarcerated in an asylum. None of this, of course, was true. It was nothing but malicious gossip spread by word of mouth, although, in the circumstances, it assumed the guise of truth. It induced the authorities to put me under observation, and I returned to our small town branded by madness. This is the sequence of events:

After a wonderful early spring spent at San Geminiano and Siena, I arrived in Rome just before Easter, at a time when the swallows were twittering around the belfries and everything was in fragrant bloom, in full Easter glory. One could see flying pigeons' shadows and hear the mysterious fluttering of birds' wings in the dark chiaroscuro of places of worship, as if everything outside that is ugly, wicked, and disgusting in human life had been obliterated.

Instead of testifying to its eternity, Rome was assuring everyone that nothing was stable, that everything was transient, would disappear and vanish irrevocably, sink in time like the shadows of the pigeons' wings on the windowpane. The massive wax candle above the grave of a pope smokes vertically and sootily like an omen. Rome was at every step the most disturbing proof that an altar has never been built that has not been destroyed. Time plays with churches as it does with all creations of man, and carries them into the clouds as the wind plays with autumn leaves. All human efforts vanish into space as does the dust on the roads along which man passes with the conviction that a human being's path is specially chosen according to a higher meaning. Man is deceived in his most fundamental assumption that the purpose of life centers on him or his prejudices.

Rome proves with every one of its bricks that in the history of human endeavor there has never been a single person who has not been endangered; who has existed only as long as he possessed the strength to defend himself. Roman architecture is nothing but a piling of ramparts, the erection of towers and steeples, the fixing of weather vanes, the fluttering of flags. From the Pantheon to the church of Propagation, all saints and Roman gods, all graves, all monuments, and all Roman sacrificial altars—everything passes as if by a flood, everything is constantly threatened by a new flood that rises with the vigor of a tidal wave, carrying all in its torrent, about which Petrarch wrote in *I Trionfi*. And what more, after Petrarch, can be said about the victory of time over man? Eternal Rome, that Palatine residence of high imperial dignitaries of divine origin, is today a city of tedious moonlight and operettas intended for the foreigners who meander through that ancient cemetery of Europe like the goats that have grazed through the centuries on Monte Caprino, since the days when the name had no meaning except what it was: a pastureland for goats.

In Rome I felt above it all, as if I were observing modern times in retrospect, watching them in the light of the barbaric centuries that are approaching us. My feeling of balanced and calm resignation excluded the possibility of any special irritation and especially of the mental incompetence that has been ascribed to me: that I had jumped up on an altar at the Sistine Chapel and injured a distinguished English lady with a heavy silver candelabrum.

The morning of that rather disgraceful incident at the Sistine Chapel, I was, objectively speaking, more sleepy than irritated. It was April, in full splendid sunshine outside and, inside the church, twilight: one-third of the ceiling was concealed behind scaffolding and tarpaulin, and up there, above our heads, a painter was whistling a tango. I sat at the front of the church behind railings, watching Galatians, Teutons, and other barbarians jostling one another like bipeds at the Last Judgment. For centuries great processions of people have passed in front of the painting above the altar; provincial chaplains with breviaries and binoculars; shortsighted English

spinsters enjoying their small annuities; a dwarfish woman; a goitrous monster.

The barbarians passing in front of Michelangelo's paintings wear
the most diverse insignia of their "outlooks on life," which they
sport like flowers in their buttonholes: tricolors, fascios, swastikas,
stars, globes, lilies, crosses, all symbols of our confused times, which
have neither an intellectual nor a moral nor an aesthetic aspect. Our
times produce chamber pots and fountain pens, with one thing in
mind only—to make as many of them as possible, as cheaply as
possible, and as profitably as possible. Christ's ideas are being
preached by means of brass bands and Boy Scout uniforms, with
drums and cymbals and banners, like some sort of military, Spartan,
physical exercise. Our times systematically ridicule everything that
is human in a human being. According to a higher plan, our times
destroy human impulses in the individual. And where are all these
people traveling to, with their enamel symbols in their buttonholes?
Why are they divided into classes and sub-classes according to their
"outlooks on life"? What are they looking for here at the Sistine
Chapel?

In the background of the picture above the altar, an enormous
flood of light, blue and dark ocher and brown, falls downward, like
a waterfall dragging with it a fleet of ships into the bottomless
abyss, the precipice gaping behind the altar, the inferno. In the bewitched flow of that diabolical stream, the flesh of a whole naked
mankind falls into nothingness.

Outside, the swallows twitter. The shadows of the pigeons fall
over the lead-framed windows. It is a sunny morning in Rome, but
here it is cold as in a cellar. Here the barbaric hoofs of those tourists thunder as they jostle one another like horned animals.

When entering the chapel, one is offered a spectacle of infinite
magnitude. What's to be seen on those walls reveals such creative

potentialities that here one may indeed be inclined to start believing that life may after all have a deeper meaning than commercial correspondence or wars generated through the intricate game of conflicting interests. Here life has come to a halt, simple yet impenetrable, as are tears, rain, clouds, and stars. How was that rheumatic, asthmatic, afflicted, abandoned, lonely, despised man able to create that? How could he dare? How did he know?

Whatever the answer, one senses one thing clearly: the man from whose mind this chaotic vision emanated did not purchase his "outlook on life" in a dime store, but came into this chapel like a meteor and left behind him the smell of cosmic sulphur. . . . And century after century men come here bleating like goats, staring wide-eyed at these testimonies of human passion and intelligence. . . .

The tourists murmur intrusively, rudely, without the least sense of dignity; they hop, sing, giggle, laugh, whistle, shout something to one another, wave their hands, binoculars, glasses, mirrors, books; they behave as if they are at a fair, on their way back to their Hottentot marsh swamps, to their barbaric stables, to their petit-bourgeois thefts, to their murders. . . .

All of a sudden I found myself accosted.

"Oh, Doctor, it's you? What are you doing here?"

"I am watching the goats."

"Really? Wonderful. . . . You enjoy art? Who would imagine that? What a strange coincidence. . . ."

It was Golombek with his wife—the director-general of a factory that made double-fat special Swiss cheese named Elvira, the fat Karl Golombek with his fat wife Elvira. This couple had no particular reason to be especially kind to me since, if they judged by my expression, it was perfectly evident I was not pleased with this unexpected encounter. I realized that neither of them was going to do me the honor of shaking hands with me. Karl Golombek peppered me immediately with a mass of questions like a detective's. When had I arrived in Rome? Where was I staying? How long would I stay? Where had I come from? Had I received any mail from home? Who was I still in touch with? Was I abreast of the latest events? Where had I been earlier? Which way had I come? What had I been doing? What were my plans? Did I intend to travel any farther? Was it true that I was going to America?

"America? Why America?"

He had read in the papers that I was escaping to America. That, at least, was what the police authorities assumed, so a man-wanted circular for me had been sent out. The police had posted the circular because I was suspected on well-founded grounds of being in touch with a shrewd band of bank-note forgers. . . .

Why did I pretend that nothing was of any concern to me? A gentleman who did not imagine he was a suspect would not play the role of neuropath or art-lover, but would—provided he had a clear conscience—place himself at the disposal of the authorities, would at least report to the consulate. . . .

"It is all based on a false assumption. It is undoubtedly an error. . . . I am permanently in touch with Dr. Kaminski, and Dr. Kaminski knows my address. . . ."

"You see that you have been telling lies. You see you've been contradicting yourself all along. What Dr. Kaminski? Now, all of a sudden? A minute ago you yourself admitted you had not received any news from home for at least a month. . . . These are all sheer tricks, my dear man."

"Karl, for God's sake, don't get on my nerves. It is none of your business anyhow."

"How do you mean it's none of my business? It concerns every law-abiding citizen. The legation should be informed right away. . . ."

I felt a deep need—in fact, a bodily need—to turn around and run and rid myself of this boor. But, on the other hand, I was disturbed by the notion that the idiot could really believe I was a forger at large for whom a circular had been sent out. I therefore tried to use logic and act accordingly. . . .

"You read in the papers that a wanted circular has been sent out for me? When?"

"When? What a funny question. It was exactly three weeks ago."

"I see. Three weeks ago. And it was stated in the papers that I was suspected of being a bank-note forger?"

"It was not reported that you personally were a forger. Not that, but that you were in touch with forgers."

"Oh! And you personally believe I am really in touch with forgers?"

"To tell the truth, why not? A man who reached for a revolver against his benefactor? A man who has been in jail. . . . You know how it is. . . . In case of need . . . please . . ."

I turned around to leave, but Golombek prevented me from retreating by his imposing butcherlike appearance.

"Why are you so frightened? Why are you trembling? Don't be afraid. I am not going to report you to the police. As far as I am concerned, you may leave freely. But have you no shame?"

I slapped his eyeglasses with my hand, right on his nose; and both he and I were instantly stained with blood. We were surrounded by custodians, matrons, guides, children, friars, Jesuits, armed guards, carabineers. Commotion on the staircases and in the corridors of the Vatican! A cut vein on the nose of Director-General Karl Golombek, the glasses of his pince-nez on my right palm, bloodstained handkerchiefs, bloodstained absorbent cotton from a first-aid cupboard at the Vatican police station, the smell of alcohol, bandages on the nose, under the soft touch of a nice-looking nurse;

and then a detailed interrogation by Friar Giacomo of the Society of
Jesus, who introduced himself to me as di Aquaforte et San Pedro
in Castello.

Giacomo di Aquaforte et San Pedro in Castello was accompanied
by his armed guards. Like the police chief of every sovereign state,
he was very polite, pleasant-looking, and relatively intelligent; one
could even say he performed his duty in a warm, human fashion.
I explained the whole case to him in detail and especially emphasized how really and truly sorry I was for having been compelled
just there, in that historic place that I venerated, to give vent to an
obscure animal instinct, but that unfortunately I had had no other
choice.

The noble di Aquaforte et San Pedro in Castello declared on behalf of the Vatican police that he, too, greatly regretted the whole
case, which was unique in the annals of the Papal State, but that he
would be compelled, in spite of all the respect he felt for me in my
ticklish situation, to obey a certain convention that exists between
the Papal State and the Kingdom of Italy, and to deliver me to the
carabineers who had been waiting for me in front of the door to
that room. The noble di Aquaforte et San Pedro in Castello performed his duty under the international convention and delivered
me into the hands of the carabineers of the Kingdom of Italy, and
the carabineers of the Kingdom of Italy put steel handcuffs on my
wrists and took me off in an armored car. The police station handed
me over to police headquarters, and police headquarters sent me to
the border, and at the border I was taken over by our border authorities, who then delivered me to the police, and the police, at
the request of the public prosecutor's office, to the Court, and the
Court to an asylum for observation.

10

AMONG
THE SHIPWRECKED

The whole mixed-up mess had been caused by Matko. Matko, the
owner of the tortoise named Geraldine, my ex-companion in jail, a
burglar who had spent more than seventeen years there, had
brought about the affair with a package of forged bank notes. One
day before Christmas Matko had rung my doorbell—being tempo-
rarily out of jail (between one burglary for which he spent five
years in jail and this latest affair with the forged bank notes)—to
seek my advice on one of his intricate legal problems, and on that
occasion, before leaving for an unidentified destination, he asked
me, "as a good comrade and a friend," to keep some of his docu-

ments in my safe. . . . . It was a package of manuscripts sealed by
Matko's seal, and I put the little parcel in the bottom pigeonhole of
the safe and completely forgot about it. When, around Easter,
Matko's gang was discovered, a certain assistant photographer
named Petri admitted that "of the forged bank notes of a hundred
dinars each, the whole collection was complete except for the seven
bank notes already in circulation and the eighty-five hundred notes
that had been concealed by Matko." It should be admitted that
Matko did not give in at once. But in the end he was compelled to
capitulate, and this accounts for Golombek's saying I was suspected
of being the accomplice of a gang of bank-note forgers, that I was
abroad, and that a circular had been sent out for me. Immediately,
the same morning, when the frontier guards had delivered me to
the authorities, a search of my apartment was made and Matko's
package was discovered in my safe; and although Matko loyally
confessed that he "did not tell me anything that was true" about the
contents of the package and that I believed they were nothing but
some of his personal documents, I was nevertheless retained in cus-
tody in the asylum pending trial.

Nobody was more desperate about it all than Matko himself.
Not because the whole collection of his precious papers had been
lost but because he had involved me in an adventure as unnecessary
to me, as Matko phrased it, "as a saddle to a sow." Judging by his
character, Matko was unquestionably a knight. A real gentleman.
A watchmaker's assistant who by sheer accident had been forced by
circumstance at the age of nineteen to steal a gold watch; and having *already previously* been branded a thief, he logically became a
burglar.

There are moments in everybody's life when it is possible to hear
the wheels of one's own fate squeaking. . . . It was a Saturday, and
Matko was in love with Miss Martha, a trainee at the post office

who was taking an evening course in accounting and bookkeeping, so that she could get a good job as a secretary. It was Saturday, and the next day was Sunday, and Miss Martha would appear in her dark red coat and look beautiful. A Sunday, with an excursion to the park on the outskirts of the town, sailing in a boat on a lake, swans, accordions, photographers, lemonades, the cinema. . . . It was Saturday, the thirtieth of the month, and the nineteen-year-old watchmaker's apprentice named Matko was absolutely broke (because he had already been advanced the money for that week), and so he made the fatal decision to pawn one of the gold watches left for repair—the one numbered 274b, which had to be ready in fourteen days, but not before. Unexpectedly, the owner of the watch numbered 274b turned up in the shop on Monday, around nine in the morning. He had to leave suddenly, would not be back in the foreseeable future, and wanted his watch, 274b.

The watchmaker's apprentice Matko admitted that watch 274b was in a pawnshop. He produced the certificate: 333c. He would have it back at the latest by next Saturday. . . . Denunciation. Admission. No extenuating circumstances. A watchman's apprentice who at nineteen steals watches will continue to do so, since he was born to be a thief. First sentence, three months. Then wandering, hunger, and suffering in seeking a job.

What job was to be had after an item in the newspaper had established the watchmaker's apprentice Matko as a thief?

"Ah, you are the Matko who stole the watch numbered 274b, are you not?"

"I did not steal it. I only pawned the watch on the assumption that I could get it back in time. That Saturday I had already drawn my salary in advance. It was the last day of the month. I had a fiancée. My fiancée . . ."

"It doesn't concern me that you were engaged. Do you imagine that in my jewelry shop, among masses of precious jewels, I can tolerate a thief?"

"But I have been working for you for nearly a whole year and have had the chance to steal from you a thousand times. If I were a thief . . ."

"Excuse me but please take your things, and good-by."

Closed doors, pavements, rain, summer, fall, winter, spring, again summer, fall, again the month of December. You just try to go for a walk in the slush that is customary in our country around Christmas wearing torn white tennis shoes like Matko, who had stolen the watch numbered 274b and pawned it on the assumption that he would recover it in time, and then did not keep the promise because he couldn't, and now had to atone for his mortal sin and go forever in snow storms in white tennis shoes and an old coat, with not even a shirt. . . . When one is condemned to such a death, it is natural that rebellion is born in a twenty-year-old man, that a healthy zest for life announces itself in him, and that it seems logical to him that a man who is chased like a wolf should become a wolf. . . . The first theft, the second theft, the third theft, and then, quite naturally, the legal and lawful consequences of those outbursts that were against the law. First, three years. Then, again, the same thing. Burglary in a jewelry shop. The second sentence: seven years. Again, set free, and once again the white tennis shoes walking in the snow, in freedom, the ringing of other people's doorbells, again thefts, a series of burglaries, several bold excursions abroad, specialization in burglary in jewelry shops, trafficking in jewels, the underworld, ten years, fifteen years, seventeen years for bank-note forgery. The prospects of that dangerous game: either the gallows or a great fortune abroad. More likely, the gallows.

I spent nearly two months in confinement with Matko and his

specialist in photographing hundred-dinar notes, Petri, when Dr. Kaminski, my colleague and a lawyer, managed to pull strings and have me put under observation. I have no reason to doubt the good intentions of my friend and comrade, Dr. Kaminski, but he has always been characterized by a dose of paranoia as well as by a rather moronic lack of common sense. I have never doubted this from the very first day of our acquaintance. No one has ever had any reason whatever, judging by any conduct or statement of mine, to question my common sense, but I think it is not inconceivable that during that period of observation I lost my nerve several times, first because I had no idea my comrade Dr. Kaminski was trying to get me out of trouble and, second, because the behavior of certain gentlemen toward me was such that "losing one's nerve," to put it mildly, was the least you could risk in that asylum where the authorities showed many more signs of madness than the madmen they had to observe. Had I not found Dr. Katančić, a blackmailer, a pamphleteer, and a shipwrecked man, over there behind the hospital railings of my pretrial confinement, I do not know what shape my latest adventure might have taken after my friends had put me in a strait jacket to drag me out of the fantastic consequences threatening every bank-note forger or his associates.

The case history of Dr. Katančić showed that he was a man who had lost the dignity of a citizen after he embezzled his clients' money, a politically exposed member of the central committee of a bourgeois patriotic party who was let down by his party friends because they were afraid of his abilities, which were extraordinary in every respect. This was the account of a commonplace, sad, shipwrecked man who himself represented the deep, dark, invaluable experience of our country. Personally, I did not know Dr. Katančić, and everything I had heard about him (this was during the penultimate chapter of his tragic career) was in the main scandalous: that he was immoral, lecherous, a drunkard, debauched, a blackmailer; that he wrote pamphlets to order, that he had robbed his clients and deservedly lost his advocacy, that he was a dangerous scribbler; in a nutshell: a suspicious mixture, half swindler and half bohemian—a man of artistic, frivolous nature who had ruined his family—a man, in short, who would sooner or later die like a dog. This Dr. Katančić published some semi-literate and semi-political fortnightlies. I remember when, from time to time I would have a chance to glance at some of the articles under his signature, I would be sickened by his destructive style that made me think of bedbugs leaving behind a suspicious odor, especially when touting obviously fabricated balance sheets or quoting the lofty objectives of a patriot. I knew that he had been disbarred, that he had spent two or three years in prison for embezzlement, and that he had been sentenced in our courts several times for slander; and since I considered such things from a distance (like a genuine top-hatted man, I did not think about certain things at all), I connected Katančić's appearance and signature and name with something that leaves a bad smell. From a strait jacket, however, things are seen from a different point of view, and my image of Katančić changed completely. . . . Everybody forges signatures on promissory notes, everybody receives bribes, tells lies, steals and cheats and amasses money, and only shipwrecked persons who were born as righteous men—that is, people whose nerves have been undermined to such an extent that their vital instincts have been subordinated to their brains—become rags crushed and spat on, because they do not know how to adjust themselves to the animal farm where one single rule is dominant: that the blood let out from the throat of one's neighbor is the warmest and consequently the most nourishing. . . .

"You see, I have been crushed. Why? Because I dared to oppose human folly," Dr. Ljudevit Katančić used to say, lying on his straw mattress and smoking a cigarette calmly and indifferently, as if talking about a third person. "I permitted a dullard to oppress me, because I myself was one of those stupid people, and this is the story of my shipwreck. If I had not let people crush me, but had trampled on people myself, I would have been a respected and honored citizen today. Everybody who spits on me now, who feels horrified in talking about or referring to me—all that scum would have trembled whenever I made my appearance; they would have been terrified in my presence or by my look or signature if I wanted to be a scoundrel and sit on their back. But I chose anonymous, hidden suffering; and still I am not in a position even to say that in spite of everything I have a clear conscience. For my own comfort I have the knowledge that at least fifteen times I could have settled my situation by giving up my political loyalties . . . I do not know why I didn't—I should have given in, since I didn't have the courage for the struggle. . . . In fact, if a man who plays cards loses everything, he should be bold enough to shoot himself. . . . And I embarked on that adventurous life with badly undermined nerves. Even at the beginning, I was a has-been, already a beggar. . . . Mind what I am telling you. If you want to listen to the advice of an old, experienced shipwreck then, my dear doctor and colleague, know that you, too, will be crushed, and that this is going to happen with mathematical precision. You have an unquestionable advantage over me: you are neither a fraud nor an embezzler. But even in your case they have already been applying the old recipe by blaming you as a forger, a madman, established as such in court; a police informer, a doubtful character, a paranoid, paralytic, climacteric. . . . I have been watching those snouts around us who became in turn Turkish, Albanian, German, or Hungarian supporters. My whole life I have observed renegades who have become bandits,

fouling their own ancestors, and I knew there were only a few people among us who did not surrender to comfort. As for you, my dear
Doctor, I must admit you have surprised me. . . . Truly, you have
set all the high-placed consciences of our elite against you for having dared to call attention to a common bandit and to tell him in
public he is what he is: a bandit. Whoever does not creep like a
poodle on all fours and lick hands for three glasses of wine and
soda will be crushed, uprooted, destroyed, spat on, thrown into the
mud like a dead body. Frankly, I worry about you. . . . And if I
were you, materially independent as you are, do you know what I
would do? I would sell everything I had, cash in on it, and leave."

The situation in which I found myself when granted bail in order
to prepare my defense was not so fortunate. After the first trial,
Domaćinski stood before me in his true legal regalia like an apparition in a provincial theater; the second trial was devoted to the insults and slanders unquestionably established by reliable witnesses,
speaking in favor of Domaćinski as a prominent member of the
bourgeoisie. In addition to the second trial there was a double trial
with the Rugvays for which a date had already been fixed. Moreover, there was the indictment with a semi-official significance from
the court judges and the official indictment from the public prosecutor's office for a whole series of offenses punishable under the law.
There were several minor accusations (Aquacurti-Daljski, Von
Petretich, etc.), accusations raised by the lawyers Hugo-Hugo and
Hermansky, accusations by the big industrialist Karl Golombek for
grave bodily harm, the accusation of my father-in-law, the druggist
and inventor of digestive tea, for a forged deed of gift (whereby I
was given the three-storied house at Bishop's Square as a gift), the
Matko-Petri trial for the forged bank notes, the divorce case on the
basis of accusations by my wife Agnes in which, among other

things, she accused me of abnormal sexual inclinations. In a nutshell: there was a whole wagonload of highly intricate legal matters
that could have kept busy a much larger lawyer's office than mine;
as a matter of fact, after the breach with Domaćinski, I was its only
employee and its only client.

Contemplating a pile of garbage in my mind and perusing old
private, personal mail that had accumulated since my departure for
Italy, I found a mysterious letter from Vienna. Who could have
written to me from Vienna? A light gray envelope and an unintelligent, pointed, resolute female handwriting. The address was correct,
but there was no sender's name, and the postmark was from Vienna,
early March. . . . As for the smell of the letter, it was indefinable—
it might have been wet starch. Holding it in my palm, I felt a considerable weight. What could be underneath that slightly creased
envelope? A cartoon? A photograph?

Between two sheets of hard paper (why hard paper?) was a
copy of the Vienna *Journal* announcing a suicide in the Vienna
Club. That trifling, apparently insignificant, local piece of news
from Vienna was underlined in thick red pencil. The news read:
"Suicide by a woman artist. At the nightclub where she had sung
old songs, last night, after the performance, the artist Jadviga
Jesenska poisoned herself. The cause of her suicide is unknown." On
the margin of this obituary, in the same handwriting and the same
ink used on the envelope, was written: "By the dead person's request. With respects, Nelly ——" (the surname was unreadable).

On the cold, almost polar surface of my consciousness I felt a
dull and rather flat pressure. I rose to my feet and lit a cigarette. I
strolled up and down the room two or three times and then stopped
in front of the window. It was a warm summer night. Life was
normal under the branches of the chestnuts, as if nothing special
had occurred. An ice-cream vendor was on his way home, and the sil-

very light of his acetylene lamp flooded the streets in irregular
waves, casting enormous shadows on the walls like a ship on a
rough sea. The shadows of the trees quivered down the street, and
from afar, over the roofs, one could hear the sound of a brass band
from a distant park. On the other side of the street, an empty room
in a bourgeois flat could be seen. One could not see or hear anyone
in the flat. Against the dark red carpet the pleated orange silk
shade of an enormous lamp festively illuminated the room and in
the background shone the gold frame of a dark picture. I stood at
the window for a long time without a single thought in my mind,
puffing my cigarette and contemplating the smoke spreading in flat
waves and dispersing along the window sill. Then, suddenly, a quite
unexpected and bizarre idea came to me—to switch on the radio
and seek refuge in music.

Man can hide himself, escape, disappear, unburden himself when
listening to music. He can dissolve in the sound waves of a voice,
sink and submerge in the bitter and dark amplitude of a cello, the os-
cillations of a flute. The velvet of the rest, a rain of mild sounds, the
vibrations of the veils of music, the thundering of the waterfall,
carry us along and we finish in the abyss, in starry, stormy, dark-
brown depths. . . . The ceilings soar upward, the invisible ceilings
of dark buildings; and from above flickering white and green light.
. . . Man is alone, man suffers, man walks and walks, travels, tries
to escape, to unburden himself, to hover. On the waves of obscure
echoes, he flies, leaving his body behind, and is lost within the
magic realm of his heart and blood stream. He is nothing more than
a sleepy shadow, a sad weary apparition with a cigarette in his hand,
turning like a madman the strange button onto an electric guitar
that plays on and on in an empty room where lies a copy of the
Vienna *Journal* with the obituary of Jadviga Jesenska. . . . Everything is just a gulping, but not in the direction of the intestines,

downward, forced by gravitation, but upward, underneath the glassy
arches of the brain where all roofless buildings stand open and
where everything soars upward, all movement becomes transparent,
crystal-clear, perfect and sonorous. . . .

And, a fraction to the right, locomotives, machine guns, laws,
spurs, the noise of factories, the feeling of a vacuum—a complete
vacuum both in head and in heart, the vertical axis of complete
silence around which endless and enormous darkness forms a howling whirlwind. In that dark vacuum the voice of a lecturer is heard
from space: about dogs' diseases in large cities, with special reference to the speed developed by modern means of transport. Another
voice is talking about poisonous gases and the armaments of the
superpowers. An opera, applause in a golden hall, the yellow reflection of twilight on the music, thunder in the boxes, the march of
time, one, two, one, two, the march of endless rows in thirty-three
opposite directions, one two, one two, meetings, applause, the
yelling of the mob, banners, bell-ringing, gunfire, rockets. . . . An
accordion: "Parlez-moi d'amour," and, at the same fraction's distance, a little more to the right, Madrid, Shanghai. . . . A fraction to
the left, the marching of a battalion, one two, the cracking of
sparks under the thin veneer of this magic box that plays in an
empty room; smoke, bell-ringing, fires, churches, night, and the
loneliness of a man who is nervously tapping his radio as if seeking
a connection with someone in the vacuum. A speaker's voice,
Mozart, a motif from *The Magic Flute.* Tonight the whole of Europe is dancing the fox trot, and here one man is unutterably alone,
encircled by voices—absolutely alone, listening to the crackling of
his box, the tuning of instruments prior to a performance in a
distant opera house. . . . The instruments in the twilight of a golden
hall talk like birds at the break of day in a forest, a dewy forest
above which the skies emerge so dark blue that one could easily get

lost in that forest at dawn. Copenhagen reports that the younger son of Johann Sebastian Bach, born in 1735, studied music in Bologna with Father Martini. Bach's son gave concerts in London—you should take advantage of the situation of the government in London. . . . The celebrated violinist Fritz Kreisler reports from New York that at various corners on its streets he played as a street musician more than thirty times, and none of the passers-by ever took any notice of him or realized it was a virtuoso playing—the voice of a siren, searchlights, elegant fashion, tennis matches; ticktock, ticktock, fifteen-forty, match—bravo—the conductor banging his baton on the podium, the birds from the forest can no longer be heard: hush, calmness prevails, except for an old bon vivant coughing in the front row of the pit. Hush, the cantilena is slowly extinguished like the twilight, ticktack, ticktack thunders the machine gun above the muddy trench; the noise of sirens, a whistle on the railroad—the journey is a mad one; the waves whistle, the wind howls; the sea glitters, the boats swing in a mild north wind, the clock strikes noon. . . .

Midnight. The clock from Westminster Cathedral strikes. Someone must have died. A quiet violin sings about waterfalls, about naked female elbows in a crowded hall, and a female alto soars from a nightclub. It is late at night. A cigarette burns in the corner of the pianist's lip, strong alcohol is drunk, gongs ring, a transparent veil of sounds, a glittering dewy moonlight, enormous, dark piles of melancholy chords. . . .

The dark. At twilight the instruments unfold like flowers, the dark-brown pitchy lava flows, craters of lava smoke, someone pathetically talks about the international balance of power. Little bells ring. The organ plays. The waltz from *The Merry Widow:* "Let's go to Maxim's". . . . If one could just sleep. Fall asleep.

Certainly and forever. Not to be.